EMBRACE THE DARK

HER ELEMENTAL DRAGONS BOOK FIVE

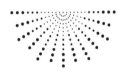

ELIZABETH BRIGGS

For all the children trying to make their parents proud

CHAPTER ONE

Some people had no idea they were destined for greatness. I'd spent my entire life preparing for it—and today my destiny was supposed to begin.

Nervous, excited energy woke me before the sun. After tossing and turning for an hour, I accepted that falling back asleep was futile, so I rose with the dawn and dressed in my combat leathers. My Ascension wouldn't happen until this afternoon, which meant I had many hours to fill until then. Burning off some energy was the only way I'd get through the longest day of my life.

My steps echoed along the white marble halls of Soulspire Palace, and I nodded to the few guards I passed. The morning's silence melted away as I neared the kitchen, which was already bustling with activity as the staff prepared for the banquet tonight in my honor.

The head chef gave me a bright smile and offered me a warm blueberry muffin. "Happy birthday, Sora," she said, and a chorus of echoes went up around the room from the other cooks and servers.

"Thank you," I told everyone, before shoving half the muffin in my mouth. Fresh out of the oven and delicious. Another young woman offered me a glass of milk, which I chugged down.

"Would you like us to make you some breakfast? An omelet, perhaps?" Hada asked.

"No, but thank you." I grabbed an apple off a nearby tray on my way out the door. My stomach was too twisted to eat much of anything, and I doubted I'd be able to sit still long enough for a full meal anyway.

I crunched down on the apple as I headed outside into the fresh, cool air. Clouds gathered overhead, but otherwise it was a beautiful morning, the kind that made you feel like the day could only bring good things. I headed past the garden my mother created to the training grounds, where dozens of soldiers were already sparring with each other. I scanned the area for one of my fathers, Jasin, who led the Silver Guard, the elite fighting force dedicated to serving the Dragons. I didn't spot him there, but I did see someone else who made me smile.

Erroh caught my eye and grinned before jogging over to me. I tried not to admire the way his muscular body looked in his soldier's uniform and dragged my gaze back to his face instead. Not that it helped, since his face was just as appealing. His dark hair was cut military-style, showing off his chiseled cheekbones, golden-brown skin, and warm eyes. He was the spitting image of his father, Cadock, except with the coloring of his mother, Faya. Both Cadock and Faya worked for my parents, with Cadock acting as Jasin's second in command, and Faya handling diplomacy with my other father, Auric. Erroh was only a few months older than me, and since he'd also grown up in the palace—along with his older siblings Daka and Parin—he'd been my best friend for as long as I could remember.

"Happy birthday," he said as his arms circled me. I leaned into his embrace for probably a little too long. As we pulled back, our faces turned toward each other and our lips were close, way too close. For a second we paused, tempted to close the gap, but then we broke apart and looked away quickly. We both knew the Gods would choose my four mates later today. Erroh and I could never be together. Not as anything more than friends, at least.

He cleared his throat and rubbed the back of his neck. "I can't believe it's finally here."

"Me neither." I couldn't meet his eyes. The moment had grown awkward, as it always did whenever we spoke of such things. If I were any other girl, without a Gods-ordained destiny, we'd probably already be married.

"I'm guessing you couldn't sleep and that's why you're out here so early," he said. He knew me so well.

I nodded. "I thought I might have a run through the Gauntlet to burn off some energy. Care to join me?"

Erroh glanced behind him at the other soldiers, but his sparring partner had moved on to someone else. He turned back and grinned at me. "You know I never miss a chance to be humiliated by the Ascendant."

I nudged him in the arm. "You might beat me this time."

"On your big birthday? I wouldn't dare."

We passed the soldiers' training area and headed around the buildings toward an elaborate training course where I often practiced running, jumping, and climbing. The Silver Guard used it also, but it had originally been designed for me by my four fathers. The soldiers called it the Gauntlet, and running it successfully was one of their major tests. I'd been doing it since I was seven.

We climbed up the ladder to the first platform, where we had a perfect view of the rising sun making the sky the color of pink roses. The Gauntlet spread before us, with different platforms and various challenges all designed to test my skills. I tied my wild, curly brown hair back in a tight bun and shook out my limbs. "Ready?"

Erroh finished stretching out his arms and nodded. "First one to the finish line has to get the loser a present."

I cocked my head at him. "I'm not sure that's how winning is supposed to work."

He shrugged and then took off, leaping from the platform to grab onto the zipline overhead. He zoomed down it, and I cursed him under my breath and hopped onto the zipline right after him. He hit the ground on the next platform with me only seconds behind him, and then we both ducked down under the first obstacle and scrambled over the next one.

My focus narrowed to my own movements as I jumped across small steps over a pool of water, before climbing up to another platform. From here I carefully crossed the rope walkway suspended over the same pool of water, belly crawled through a dark moss-covered tunnel, and then wove my way through thick forest and large rocks until I reached the next platform. We kept going, racing through the course and overcoming other obstacles, including huge swinging stones I had to dodge between, holes in the ground that randomly shot bursts of fire or water, and an area with heavy wind that could knock you over if you weren't careful.

Finally we reached the last platform, this one a steep rock hill with only a few handholds, made by my other father Slade with his earth magic. I climbed it while breathing heavily. Only then did I notice Erroh again beside me, and we pulled onto the platform at the same time. We both leaped across and grabbed onto the rope hanging before us, then swung to the next one and grasped it, and kept going like this until we reached the other side. I got there only seconds before him and sprinted over the random obstacles in the way, until I reached the end. I grabbed the white flag and raised it triumphantly, while Erroh came to a halt beside me. We both bent over and tried to catch our breath, sweat dripping from our brows.

"I let you win," he said.

"Sure you did." I threw the balled-up flag at his chest. "If you're expecting a present for losing, forget it."

He grinned and hung the flag back in its spot. "Ah well, it was worth a try."

We climbed down the platform and sat on the grass to stretch our legs and calm our racing hearts. I wiped sweat off my forehead and leaned back, gazing at the clouds gathering overhead. For those few minutes on the Gauntlet my mind had been blissfully clear, but now the thoughts slowly crept back in. Today I was twenty years old. Today I would be blessed by the Gods so I could take my mother's place as the Silver Dragon. Today my life would change forever.

"What distraction do you need now?" Erroh asked, breaking me out of my fog. "Shall we get our swords? Throw some knives? Head into town and drink some ale at a seedy tavern?" He waggled his eyebrows at this.

I laughed. "You should probably get back to your own training. I might run the Gauntlet a few more times though."

"Whatever you want," Erroh said with a grin. "I'll just have to get you drunk at the banquet instead."

"That sounds good. I'll need to be drunk to deal with all the stuffy noblemen and diplomats. Speaking of, is your brother going to be there?"

"No, Parin is still on assignment in the Earth Realm. I'm sure he sends his best wishes and all that." Erroh stood up and brushed the grass off his uniform. "Daka isn't coming either, unfortunately. The baby is still too young for them to travel. But I'll be there representing the family, don't you fret."

"Thank goodness for that." I stood up and almost reached for him, but then stopped myself. "Thanks for the distraction today, and for being so understanding about... everything. I know it hasn't always been easy, but I'm glad you're my best friend."

His jaw clenched a little, but he smiled. "I'll always be there for you, Sora. You know that." He leaned forward and pressed a kiss to my forehead. "Good luck today."

He walked away and I allowed myself to check out his behind one last time. In a few hours the Gods would choose my mates, and then I'd only have eyes for them. But for now I could at least admire my first love a little longer.

After running the Gauntlet until my muscles twitched and sweat ran down my body, I finally returned to the palace. I stopped in the kitchen to grab a drink and some food, but paused when two familiar faces rounded the corner ahead of me. They abruptly halted when they saw me, and one of them gave me a charming smile, while the other had on a permanent frown. Carth and Zain, total opposites, and yet somehow best friends. They were also two of the most handsome men I'd ever seen.

Carth was dressed in fine silks that brushed across his tan skin, the soft yellow and pale blue marking him as a nobleman from the Air Realm. His sandy hair always looked windswept, and his sea green eyes and muscular swimmer's body hinted at his origins in the Water Realm. When he was four years old, his family was on a boat that was lost in a storm. Water elementals rescued him and brought him to Soulspire, where he was adopted by Brin, a friend of my parents, and Leni, my aunt. That made Carth my adopted cousin, which made my desire for him rather awkward. It didn't help that Carth was an incessant flirt either.

Zain wore the black and red armor of a guard of the Fire Temple, and his eyes were the blue of the hottest part of a flame. His grandmother was the former High Priestess Calla, who helped my mother during her time as Ascendant. Calla was like a grandmother to me too, and that made Zain sort of like an older, protective brother to me. He was always serious and somewhat aloof when I was younger, though his eyes were always on me. As I grew older, the looks he gave me changed and became something different, something that made my heart race. Last time I saw him was a year ago, when we shared a secret, passionate kiss against the outside wall of the Fire Temple, his fingers skimming across my breast. After that, we never spoke again. The whole encounter confused and excited me, even though I'd tried my best to put it out of my mind.

"Hey there, birthday girl," Carth said, before wrapping a

tan, muscular arm around my shoulders. "How are you feeling? Excited? Nervous?"

"Both those things, and many more as well," I admitted.

"But mostly excited to meet your mates, I imagine." Carth pressed a hand to his chest dramatically. "Oh, that I could be one of them."

Did he? Or was he being dramatic? I could never tell with Carth. I'd secretly longed for the same thing for years, but my mother's mates were all strangers, so I'd never held out much hope it would happen.

Zain lifted his chin. "The Gods know what they are doing, and will pick the best men for the role."

Carth nudged his friend. "Sure, but wouldn't it be nice if she got to pick? Or at least could tell them her preferences?"

"We do not question the will of the Gods," Zain said sternly. Then he rested a warm hand on my elbow. "Just know that whatever happens, we will always watch out for you."

"I'm sure I'll be happy with their selection," I managed to say, as heat crept up my neck from the two men's touches. Both of them had always been there for me my entire life, but I was sure things would change between us after today.

"If not, you can always come to me on the side. I'll make sure you're well taken care of." Carth gave me a wink, while Zain rolled his eyes. "See you at the banquet tonight."

They continued on their path, and I let out a sigh while I watched them go, admiring their muscular physiques and the way they moved. Two more men who were completely off-limits because of who I was. Carth had asked the same questions I'd had my entire life, but I'd always been afraid to admit them out loud. How did I know the Gods would really choose my best mates? They'd done a good job with my mother, but what if things were different for me?

Why didn't I get any say in my own future?

CHAPTER TWO

Finally, it was time.

I made my way to my mother's garden, which she'd created before I was born in honor of the Life Goddess. As I walked along the path, I noticed a white rose had been trampled into the stone, and bent down beside it. I brushed my fingers across the wilted petals and gave a little push, and the flower lifted up and healed thanks to the energy I gave it. Once the rose was as good as new, I continued into the garden.

My parents were all waiting there among the verdant leaves and colorful flowers, but otherwise we were alone. I stepped toward them as storm clouds gathered overhead, threatening rain at any moment. One by one my fathers gave me a hug and wished me a happy birthday. Slade, my father by blood, came to me first, his dark eyes proud as he gave me a big bear hug. He was a very large man, and as a kid there was nowhere safer than on his lap, especially when he'd read me a book in his deep voice. Jasin was next, and he lifted me up and spun me around like I was still his little girl. He'd always been the fun dad who used to make messy art with me out in the courtyard with paint and pastels, although he'd been serious about my combat and military training. Then came Auric, who rested his hands on my shoulders and gave me a kiss on the cheeks, before wiping a tear from the corner of his wise gray eyes. Auric always encouraged my imagination with dolls and miniature horses and dress-up parties, and at night he would read me stories until his voice was hoarse. Finally came Reven, whose face showed no emotion until he pulled me against him and whispered in my ear, "Good luck, kid." The sentiment in his voice made my chest tighten as I hugged him back. Sometimes I felt I was more like Reven than anyone else, even though we shared no common blood. He'd taught me all my favorite things, from lock picking to throwing knives to parkour, and he always gave me space to be myself.

My four fathers stepped back, and my mother, Kira, moved closer and embraced me. She smelled like fresh jasmine and her hug was warm and comforting as I buried my face in her red hair. As I pulled back, the sky darkened, the clouds blocking the sun.

"Your twentieth year is finally here." Mom smiled wistfully and glanced at her mates. "I don't think any of us are ready."

"I am." I straightened my shoulders. As of today I was an

adult, and soon I would be mated with four men so I could begin to take my mother's place as guardian of the world. I'd prepared for this moment my entire life and I was ready for it...wasn't I? A flicker of doubt made my stomach churn. "Will it hurt?"

"Only a little," Mom said.

I nodded. Kira had gone through this without any training. She'd had no idea she was the Ascendant, and had been shocked and confused by what had happened to her—what was about to happen to me. Unlike her, I'd had five people prepare me for this moment, and I was going to face it bravely.

"Don't worry. You can handle it." Mom smoothed back my wild curls as she gazed into my hazel eyes, which mirrored her own. "I'm so proud of you. I know you're going to do great things."

I drew in a breath and stood a little taller. "Thanks, Mom. I have a big legacy to live up to, but I'll do my best."

"I know you will." She kissed my forehead, and then returned to stand with my fathers a short distance away. There was nothing more they could do for me now. I was on my own.

Slade began pacing back and forth, and I heard my parents start to murmur quietly to each other, no doubt fussing over me in their own way. I could only make out a few words, but it sounded like they were plotting to deal with my mates if they ever hurt me. I pitied my future mates a little—they had no idea what was about to happen to them, or that they'd have to live with my four overprotective fathers. At least Mom never had to deal with that.

As I waited and nothing happened, I started to wonder if we'd gotten the time wrong. Auric had unearthed an old book in the palace from back before the Black Dragon—my grandmother—had ruled, and it had laid out the basics for the Ascension. It would occur exactly twenty years after the moment of the Ascendant's birth, which should be right now. And yet...nothing.

Hurry up already, I told the Gods.

I crossed my arms and called out, "How long am I supposed to wait?"

"I'm sure it will be soon," Mom said.

I huffed and raised my eyes to the sky, just as rain began to pour down on me, as if the Gods had heard my plea. Within seconds, I was soaked. I started to call out again, and that's when the lightning bolt shot down from the clouds and hit me.

The words in my throat turned to a silent scream as my whole body stiffened. Energy coursed through me, crackling with power, and I spread my arms wide as if it might shoot out of me and relieve the pressure—but that didn't help. Wind swirled around me and lifted me into the air, embracing me with its magic, and then I dropped down hard into the mud. I was covered from head to toe in it, and all I could do was kneel as the magic overwhelmed me. Slowly it receded and the rain slowed to a light drizzle.

I lifted my head. As I did, I felt a strange unease in my

stomach, and darkness spread out from me in a circle, turning the grass and plants brown. Leaves and petals fell and shriveled up into dust, leaving only hard branches behind. The circle of death stopped just before it hit my parents, and then the magic disappeared and the sun peeked through the clouds again.

"What was that?" I asked, as I rose to my feet. My limbs felt weak, like I'd just run for miles, and something wasn't right. Mom had never mentioned a ring of death when she told me the story of her own Ascension.

"I don't know," Kira said, her face troubled. "Auric?"

He shook his head. "I've never read about anything like that happening before."

Reven's fists clenched. "It has to be the Death Goddess."

"You think she's making her presence known?" Jasin asked.

Slade growled. "Is she tries to harm Sora, we will defeat her again."

Mom bent down and touched the ground, and the grass and plants all returned to life, as if it had never happened. "It's probably nothing," she said, as she brushed dirt off her hands. "However, we will send out extra patrols tonight in case more shades return, to be safe."

I nodded, though I had a feeling she was only saying that to keep me calm. Something wasn't right and we all knew it, but we weren't sure exactly how bad it was yet. All I knew was that my family would be with me to face whatever the problem was…along with my new mates, who I should be meeting soon.

That night there was a banquet in my honor celebrating my twentieth birthday and my Ascension. The day marked the beginning of my parents' retirement, and the start of the next dragon cycle. Important people from all four Realms, plus the elementals' home Divine Isle, all came to give me gifts and wish me a happy birthday, either to size me up or try to earn my favor. It should have been a joyous occasion for me, but I found myself distracted all evening as I thought about what happened during my Ascension.

It didn't help that Erroh was missing from the banquet either, along with Carth and Zain. I knew things would change between us after this day, but I still hoped we could all be friends. Perhaps knowing my mates had been chosen for me was too hard for them. I understood that, but I still felt like a part of me was missing all evening, and every time I glanced at their empty seats my chest ached. Whatever happened to Erroh getting me drunk tonight?

I made an excuse to head to bed as soon as I could without being rude. Mom gave me a knowing smile. "Ready to dream of your mates?" she asked, as she kissed me on the cheek.

I nodded. It was time to move on to the men who *would* be there for me. "I'm anxious to meet them."

She smoothed a wayward piece of curly hair on my head. "Me too. I'm sure the Gods have chosen well."

I could only hope she was right, even as I wondered what the Death Goddess could be planning. Whatever it was, it couldn't be good.

It took me forever to fall asleep, but once I did, the dream came, just as Mom told me it would. She'd seen Jasin first, and since he was the first of her mates to arrive and the first she bonded with, I had to assume the man I dreamed of would be my first as well.

The man in my dream had straight black hair that hung past his shoulders and shone like ink, and a face that looked familiar, though I couldn't place it. He wore no shirt, and I admired his impressive broad shoulders and muscular chest. Tattoos ran down both his arms, and though I couldn't make them out too well in the dream, I spotted one with a skull.

A wicked grin spread across his handsome face, and I only saw cruelty in his pale eyes. He looked down at a man kneeling before him, and then grabbed him by the neck and lifted him up in the air. The poor man flailed and kicked, while my future mate laughed and held him with one hand —an impressive show of strength. All the life drained out of the man, and the black-haired fiend dropped the body to the floor with a smirk. He brushed off his hands, as if wiping off a bit of dust on them, and then turned away.

I woke with a start and a lump of dread in my stomach. How could that man—that *murderer*—be one of my mates?

Who had the Gods chosen for me?

CHAPTER THREE

The next morning, I woke late. I'd tossed and turned so much that once sleep finally took me, it didn't want to let me go. I slowly bathed and dressed, remembering the strange, deadly man in my dream, and wondering about the other men I might dream of next. As I pulled on a casual green gown and tied back my wild hair, I stared at myself in the mirror, at my light brown skin and hazel eyes.

Today I was a new person—the Ascendant. Yet I didn't feel any different. I was still just Sora. Daughter of heroes. Child to four fathers. Girl with an inescapable destiny.

I headed to the small dining room where my family often shared an informal meal together, wondering if I would find any traces of breakfast. A few pieces of fruit and bread remained, and I put together a small plate. A servant rushed in and offered to make me something, but I declined. She returned anyway with some juice and scrambled eggs, because the staff always took good care of me. I thanked her profusely and then sat down to eat in the quiet room.

As soon as I took the first bite, the door burst open and Erroh rushed inside. "There you are!" he said, as he came toward me. "I've been looking for you."

He seemed excited to see me for some reason, but all I could think of was how he'd skipped my birthday banquet. "Is that so?"

He slid into the chair beside me. "I have something to tell you."

I raised an eyebrow as I stabbed my fork into my eggs. "Is it an explanation for where you were last night?"

"Yes, actually. I'm very sorry about that, but something happened. Something incredible." He drew in a deep breath. "The Air God came to me."

I dropped my fork. "What?"

His eyes danced with barely-contained excitement. "Sora, I'm one of your mates. Can you believe it?"

"No, I can't." I stared at him, and he gazed back with sincerity. Was it possible? All of my mother's mates had been strangers, so I assumed mine would be as well. "Is this a joke of some kind?"

"Definitely not. Watch." He waved his hand, and a huge gust of wind hit the flower vase on the table and knocked it over, spilling water everywhere. He jumped up and righted it immediately. "Oops, I did not mean to do that. I have a lot to learn, obviously."

I let out a surprised laugh. Erroh was one of my mates!

My first one, at that. Tears of joy hit my eyes and I jumped up to throw my arms around him. He hugged me back hard, and then our lips met without any hesitation. He kissed me with so much passion it made my heart race, and relief swept through my entire body. Kissing Erroh felt natural and so right, and now I could do it for the rest of my life without guilt or worry. I didn't have to give him up after all.

"You have no idea how much I prayed for this," Erroh said, as he pressed his forehead against mine. "I've loved you my entire life, and I couldn't stand the thought of not being with you. I begged the Gods to choose me, and the Air God listened."

"I always loved you too, but I didn't think it was possible for you to be my mate, so I never let myself hope." I let out a long breath and laughed softly. "Oh, this makes me feel a lot better."

He pulled back and studied me. "What do you mean? Is something wrong?"

I hesitated, but there was no hiding anything from Erroh, my best friend for my entire life. And now my mate. "My dream last night... I'm sure it's nothing."

His brow furrowed. "You didn't dream of me?"

"No. I should have, but it was someone else."

"Perhaps everyone's Ascension is different. So much was lost during your grandmother's rule. For all we know, it happened much differently for her than for your mother."

His calm voice always settled my nerves. I smiled. "Yes,

I'm sure you're right. If the Gods chose you, they must know what they're doing."

The door opened again, and Carth strolled inside with a big cocky grin, followed by a more serious Zain, with eyes that smoldered as they landed on me. The instant they arrived, my knees grew weak, and I grabbed onto the nearby table to steady myself. I suddenly knew why they'd also missed my banquet—they'd been chosen too.

"Let me guess, Water and Fire?" I managed to ask, though I was suddenly breathless.

"How did you know?" Carth asked.

I pressed a hand to my spinning head. "All three of you missed my banquet last night. Erroh was chosen by the Air God. It only makes sense you were chosen by Water and Fire. I just can't believe it's possible."

"It's a great honor to be chosen by one of the Gods," Zain said. "And now we can continue protecting you, as we've always done."

Carth nodded. "It makes sense. The three of us have always looked after you your entire life. We've always been your closest friends. Who else would the Gods choose but us?"

When he put it like that, perhaps it did make sense. They said the Gods always chose the best mates for the Ascendant, and maybe they looked into my heart and saw how much I cared for these three men, even though I'd tried to deny my feelings my entire life. Now I didn't have to do that anymore, and it was a huge relief. My last and final mate, my future Earth Dragon, would no doubt be a stranger, but that would be all right. I'd have my three oldest friends by my side through whatever came next.

I gave Carth a hug and kissed his cheek, and then did the same for Zane. Both of them let their hands linger on me, igniting heat between my thighs. "I'm so happy you were both chosen. Truly."

"Now we just need to wait for your final mate and then we can start visiting the temples," Erroh said, with a wide grin.

"I'm sure we're all looking forward to that," Carth said, his smile turning naughty.

I glanced between the three of them. "Are you all okay with this—with sharing me?"

"I always knew it was your destiny," Erroh said. "I'm just glad I get to be one of your mates."

Carth shrugged. "Doesn't bother me. The more the merrier."

"I was raised by four fathers," Zain said. "I understand the dynamics of it."

I let out a relieved sigh. "Good. All I can hope now is that they've chosen well for my fourth mate."

I thought back to my dream. That black-haired man must be the one chosen by the Earth God. Perhaps I didn't have dreams of these three because I already knew them?

My mother walked in, along with my father Slade. "We heard you were having a late breakfast," Mom said. "Did you have a restless night dreaming of your mates?"

I glanced quickly at the three men. "Something like that."

"I'm sure they'll be arriving soon," Slade said, as he grabbed a piece of bread.

"Actually, three of them already have." I gestured to Erroh, Carth, and Zain. "The Gods have chosen them for Air, Water, and Fire."

Mom blinked at the men, her face showing obvious surprise. "Oh! How...unexpected."

Slade's brow furrowed as he studied the three men, in particular, Carth. "These are the men the Gods chose?"

Mom elbowed him in the side and smiled at me. "How nice that you already know each other. That will save you a lot of trouble."

Slade grunted and grudgingly said, "I suppose the Gods know what is best for Sora."

I knew things would be awkward between my mates and my fathers, but this was worse than I'd expected. These men had known my parents all their lives. My parents had watched them grow up beside me, from the time we were children. Now they would have to train them and watch them become my mates. We all knew what *that* involved.

Zain cleared his throat. "We're all very honored and excited to begin training with you."

"Don't expect us to go easy on you because you're Sora's friends," my other father Revan said from behind me. He was so stealthy I hadn't even heard him come in, and now he eyed Carth with disdain. "If you hurt her or break her heart, we will end your life. Painfully. And no one will find the bodies."

Mom held up a hand. "That's enough of that, Revan."

"He's right though," Slade grumbled.

"Don't worry Uncle Slade, we'll take good care of her," Carth said, then gave Slade a friendly punch in the arm. Slade growled at him in response.

"No one is going to hurt Sora," Erroh said. "We all care about her very much."

"I hope that's true...for your sakes," Revan said.

I covered my face with my hands. This was going to be a disaster.

My parents always knew this day would come, so two years ago they moved me into a separate wing of the palace in preparation. My suite had a huge living space plus an equally large bedroom, and was surrounded by four other smaller suites prepared for my mates. Each of those rooms sat empty for years...until today.

Over the course of a few hours, my three mates moved into their new suites. Each one was decorated for their element—Carth's was done in deep blue and sea green hues, Zain's in fiery red and black, and Erroh's in pale yellow and sky blue. The last room was hunter green and warm brown, still sitting empty, but not for long.

Once the three men were all moved in, we had supper

sent up so we could share a meal together in our new dining area. I gazed across the stone table at my three friends, now my three mates, marveling over how things could change so quickly for us overnight. And yet, everything about it felt *right*. These men had always been destined to be mine.

Things were already different though. Zain and Erroh were both in plain clothes, no longer wearing the uniforms of their previous stations. They were both giving up their careers to become my mates.

"I'm sorry you had to say goodbye to your previous lives," I told them, as we began to eat. "I'm sure this is a big change for all of you."

Erroh shrugged. "I only joined the Silver Guard so I could protect you and be near you. This is even better."

"I did always wonder why you joined," I said with a smile. Growing up, Erroh had always had his nose in a book, until I dragged him off on some adventure and got us both into trouble. When he'd joined the Silver Guard at eighteen it had been a total shock. Now it made a lot more sense. My heart warmed knowing he'd done it to be near me, even though he thought he could never have me. "What about you, Zain? Are you sad you had to leave the Fire Temple for Soulspire?"

Zain shook his head. "I served the Fire God at the temple, and now I serve him here. I'll miss my family, but I'm confident this is the best place for me."

"And you, Carth?" I asked. He still wore his nobleman's

finery, with his silk shirt open just enough to give me a peek of his tan, sculpted chest.

Carth let out a short laugh as he grabbed his wine. "My sister is set to inherit mother's estates, so I've always been the spare and able to do whatever I please." A sensual grin spread across his face. "And right now, that's you."

Heat spread to my cheeks and to other places in my body, reminding me of what I would soon be doing with these three men. In order to gain my elemental powers, I would have to bond with each of them at the different temples across the four Realms. Mom had told me what would happen during the bonding, but not in too many details, of course. Still, I had an idea of what to expect.

Erroh rolled his eyes. "The texts all say she has to bond with her mates in the order of their arrival, so you'll have to wait your turn. The Air Temple is first."

"Sounds like someone is eager to get started," Carth said with a smirk.

Erroh rested his hand over mine. "I've been waiting to be with Sora for a long time. I'm ready whenever she is."

Carth trailed his fingers down my forearm. "You know, I was the first one in the room after Erroh. Therefore we should head to the Water Temple after Air, isn't that right?"

Zain scowled. "You most certainly were not. I entered the room first. I knew about the order rule, and I made sure to be the first in."

Carth shook his head. "I think if you search your memory, you'll find I'm correct."

Erroh winked at me as they argued. He didn't care who went next. He would be my first.

I couldn't help but be happy it would be him. I'd been attracted to Carth and Zain for years, but Erroh I'd loved since we were kids. Now that I could allow myself to be free and honest with how I felt, I was sure of it.

As his thumb stroked my knuckles and the gazes of the men all rested on me, desire made my heart race. I was ready. Wasn't I?

CHAPTER FOUR

My mates' training began the next day, bright and early. Each of the men lined up outside in the courtyard facing their new teachers: my fathers. Zain bowed low to Jasin, who snickered in response. Carth made a joke to Revan, but his hard expression never changed. Auric clasped Erroh on the shoulder and gave him a few kind words with a smile. At least the two of them got along.

Mom was busy meeting with some elementals and had to skip this session, but promised she would try to make future ones. Slade stood beside me with his arms crossed while they began. Everyone spread out a bit for safety purposes, and then my three fathers showed off an easy move using their element. Jasin created a small flame in his hand and moved it from one palm to the other. Auric made leaves swirl around his head. Reven blasted Carth in the chest with water, making the poor guy stumble back. I pinched the bridge of my nose and hoped this wouldn't be a total disaster.

"I'm curious to see who the Earth God chose for you," Slade said.

I remembered the dark man in my dream. Last night I'd had another vision of him, this time drinking beer while he cheered someone on with a cruel smile. "Me too."

Slade must have heard something uncertain in my voice because he wrapped an arm around my shoulders. "Have faith, daughter. Everything will make sense in time."

I leaned against him, taking comfort in his warm strength. I was truly the luckiest woman in the world to have four wonderful fathers, even if it was sometimes annoying or frustrating. Or awkward, like during this training.

As we watched, Zain set fire to a small patch of grass, Carth flooded the area around his expensive shoes, and Erroh had a hard time producing another gust of wind at all. I sighed. "Were the four of you ever this bad?"

"Unfortunately yes," Slade admitted. "We didn't have anyone to teach us how to use magic either. Don't worry. They will learn quickly with our help. You will too."

I couldn't wait to have all that power under my control. As soon as I bonded with each man, I would be able to use their element. Once I had the power of all four, I could become the next great dragon leader—like my mother.

But first, I needed my final mate to arrive.

Over the next few days my mates' training continued, while I spent my time impatiently waiting for the Earth God's chosen one to arrive—and dreading the moment too. Every night I dreamed of the same black-haired man, and every night he scared me more and more.

In the evenings, my mates and I shared more meals together and tried to move from childhood friends to something more. It wasn't as easy as I'd expected. It didn't help that the men were so exhausted after training they didn't have much energy for socializing. I started to wonder if that was my fathers' plan all along.

I was practicing sword fighting with Zain and Carth to hone my skills in defending against two attackers, when Erroh rushed past. He called out, "It's Parin! He's returned from the Earth Realm!"

Zain tilted his head as he sheathed his sword. "I thought he wasn't supposed to return for another month."

Carth shrugged. "Negotiations must have gone well."

"Or very poorly," I muttered.

Parin was Erroh's older brother, and he took his name from his father, who'd died while leading the Resistance against my grandmother, the Black Dragon. Parin's mother Faya later married former bandit turned soldier Cadock, and together they had two more children, Daka and Erroh. Parin worked as a diplomat to the Earth Realm, and often traveled back and forth between there and Soulspire.

We headed over to the courtyard in front of the palace, where Parin's contingent had arrived. He'd already exited his carriage and was speaking with his brother in hushed tones. As he lifted his head, his dark eyes met mine and lingered there. I sensed something in them, something I'd never seen before.

Parin was ten years older than me, and he'd always treated me like a little sister. He'd been my first crush growing up—the incredibly handsome older brother of my best friend with rich, dark skin, even darker coarse hair, and warm eyes that missed nothing.

"Welcome back," I said.

"Thank you." He glanced at his brother with something like worry on his face, then turned back to me. "I need to speak with you. Alone."

My eyebrows darted up. "Is something wrong?"

"Not exactly."

"What's this about?" Erroh asked.

"It's not something I care to discuss in front of you. I'm sorry, brother."

"It's fine." I didn't want the two of them to fight, but I was very curious as to what this was about. "Let's go inside so we can speak privately."

Parin and I went into the palace and to one of the receiving rooms, this one decorated in soft gold tones, while Erroh waited outside.

"What did you want to speak with me about?" I asked, once we were alone. I looked up at his handsome face and swallowed. I'd rarely been alone with him before and he made me nervous in a way no one else did. All of a sudden I felt like a little kid again, with a big, embarrassing crush on an older man I could never have.

"Sora, I must tell you something." He reached out and took my hand, but with hesitation. "I am one of your mates."

My jaw fell open and I yanked my hand back, more in shock than anything else. "That's not possible."

"I assure you, it is. The Earth God came to me a few nights ago and gave me my new purpose." He paused, searching my eyes. "I do apologize for missing your birthday festivities."

"But...but..." I had so many questions and suddenly my mouth didn't seem to work right. How could all four of my mates be men I already knew? Why would they choose Erroh's brother—wouldn't that complicate things? And who was the man haunting me at night if not my fourth mate? "But my dream..."

"Your dream?" Parin asked, his brow pinching together in concern.

I shook my head, trying to clear my thoughts. "Are you sure you're my mate? I don't mean to be rude, but I'm having a hard time believing this is possible."

"I can prove it, of course." He raised a hand and the stone table beside us lifted off the ground. His control was already good, much better than the others had been at first.

It was true, then. Parin was my fourth mate.

I took a few steps backward, completely overwhelmed, and the back of my knees hit a gilded red armchair. I collapsed into it and pressed a hand to my forehead. Parin was my fourth mate. I could barely wrap my head around that as it was, but it also meant my dreams weren't leading me to him. Did this mean I had a fifth mate? No, that couldn't be possible. None of the archives had spoken of more than four mates. The dreams had to be related to something else. Something from the Death Goddess.

Something bad.

"Are you all right?" Parin asked.

I looked up at him with a weak smile. "Yes. Sorry. Just feeling a bit overwhelmed by all this."

He offered me his hand. "Understandable."

I slide my hand into his and felt a little tremor of desire as we touched. "Are you comfortable with this new role? With...being my mate?"

He shifted on his feet and looked away. "It will take some adjustment, but yes. Though I will no longer be a diplomat in the usual sense, being a Dragon will allow me to do much of my previous duties but with even more authority."

"I see...." It sounded like he was more excited about his new job than being my mate. Would he ever see me as more than a little girl?

"We must speak of Erroh." Parin's face became pained. "I realize this will be difficult for him. You may not know this, but he's always loved you. I'm not sure how to break this to him, although he must have met your other mates by now."

"He *is* one of my mates. They chose both of you. And Zain and Carth too."

He blinked in surprise. "How is that possible?"

I spread my hands, still finding it hard to believe myself. "No one knows. It seems the Gods have decided the four of you are the best mates for me."

He stroked his chin. "I suppose having Erroh as one of your mates makes this easier in some ways, and harder in others."

Definitely harder now that Parin was one of my mates too. How would I handle having two brothers as my lovers? Oddly, the idea didn't bother me, but only excited me more. I took a deep breath. "I understand things might be confusing and strange at first, but the Gods must have done this for a reason."

"Indeed." He gave a firm nod. "I suppose we must inform the others."

I swallowed. "I suppose we must."

Parin opened the door for me, but as soon as he did, we spotted Erroh right on the other side, staring at us with his face ashen.

"You heard?" I asked.

"Auric taught me how to carry sound on the wind," Erroh said absently while staring at his brother. "How could you?"

Parin held up his hands. "I did not ask for this. I'm sorry, brother."

Erroh's gaze swung to me. "Are you all right with this?"

Two gorgeous brothers I'd secretly wanted all my life were now mine. It was hard to complain, but I could tell he felt betrayed. "The Gods have chosen, and we have to trust they know what's best for us."

Parin clasped a hand on his little brother's shoulder. "I'm relieved you were chosen too. I know you've always cared for Sora."

Erroh shrugged off his touch. "I have, yes. As have Carth and Zain. But what about you?"

Parin stiffened. "I cared for her too, of course."

"Not in the same way!"

This was getting very uncomfortable. Mostly for me. I stepped between them. "Enough. You're both my mates, and you'll both have to accept that."

Erroh grumbled something, but reluctantly nodded. Parin just sighed. I could tell this was going to be a problem. What were the Gods even thinking?

CHAPTER FIVE

While servants moved Parin's belongings into his room, Erroh stood to the side with his arms crossed and watched with a scowl. I was on my way to see my mother, but stopped to nudge him in the side.

"I thought you'd be more excited to have your brother return home safely," I said.

Erroh dropped his arms and sighed. "You're right. I should be happy to see him. I'm just not sure about sharing you with him. The others, fine. But my own brother?"

"I know what you mean." I swallowed, but for me it was because the thought made my heart race. "The gods must know it'll work out."

Erroh gave me a flat stare. "You can't tell me you're excited about this. We've always avoided Parin. He's such a bore!"

I had to bite back a laugh. Was that what Erroh thought?

The truth was that I'd avoided Parin because I hadn't wanted anyone to know about my silly crush. But there was no hiding such things from the Gods, it seemed.

I gave Erroh a kiss on the cheek. "Be kind to your brother. He's just as shocked by this as you are."

He huffed. "I'll try."

My mother came down the hallway on the heels of a man carrying a big box. "You wanted to see me?"

I nodded. We stepped into my private quarters, and I shut the door behind us. "I was just about to come to your study. I thought you were in a meeting."

"I decided to come to you instead." She pushed back a strand of red hair with a smile. "Truthfully, I couldn't wait to get out of there. As soon as I got your note, I used it as an excuse to cut the meeting short."

I laughed as we headed over to the siting area beside an enormous window looking out over my mother's garden. "Was it that bad?"

Kira sank into one of the chairs and poured herself a cup of tea. "Just wait 'til you're the one who has to listen to noblemen whine about their problems all day long. Now, what did you want to talk about? Is it your mates? It's certainly odd that they're all men you already knew, but it must be nice for you too. Or at least a lot easier than mating with four strangers."

"That's not it. Not exactly." I sat across from her and twisted my hands nervously in my lap. "Did you ever dream about any men that weren't your mates?"

"No, never. Why?" She furrowed her brow and gave me her full attention.

"I've been having dreams like you did, but only of one man, and he's... He's terrifying." It was hard to say the word out loud. I wasn't scared of anything. Few people could best me at combat, and soon I would have the powers of the elements and a dragon form of my own, and then I'd be unstoppable. Possibly stronger than my mother, thanks to my lifetime of training. Yet somehow the man in my dreams unnerved me. He made me feel...vulnerable.

Mom leaned forward and studied me. "A man who isn't one of your mates?"

I nodded. "I thought he would be my fourth one, but then Parin arrived. Now I'm more confused than ever."

"You're sure he's not one of your mates? Perhaps it's a dream from the future and he has a different appearance?"

"No. I'm absolutely sure he's a different man." His appearance haunted me even while awake. Not just his appearance. His ruthlessness. His cruelty. His darkness.

I described the things he'd done in my dreams to her in a halting voice, and when I was done, Mom sat back and sighed.

"This is very unusual. I'll have your fathers look into it. I would help too, but there have been reports of missing elementals in the area and I want to investigate them imme-diately. I'm sure Auric or Reven will find something about your dreams though." She reached across and took my hand. "Don't worry. We'll figure this out."

"I can't help but be worried. The Death Goddess must be involved somehow."

"If she is, we'll confront her together. I defeated her once before, after all. She has no chance against the two of us and all our mates."

I let out a long breath, hoping she was right. "They're not my true mates yet. Not until we go to the temples and bond. I'd like to get started on that right away, especially if we'll need to face the Death Goddess. We can head to the Air Temple tomorrow even."

Mom frowned and studied my face. "You don't need to rush into this. Focus on your mates. Get to know them."

"I already know them. I grew up with them, after all."

"It's different now that they're your mates, and not just your childhood friends. Your relationship with them needs time to flourish and grow."

"We might not have time," I grumbled.

"You have plenty of time. Your fathers and I are in no hurry to step down. We'll only do so when we're sure you and your mates are ready for the responsibility." She ruffled my curls a little. "Patience, my love."

I sighed. Patience never was one of my strong suits.

At dinner that night, I tried to follow my mother's advice.

"Let's all try to get to know each other better," I said, once we were eating. The chefs had made one of my favorite dishes from the Air Realm, with chicken, bell pepper, lemon, and cheese, layered on thin pasta. "Which meal is your favorite: breakfast, lunch, or supper?"

"Dessert," Carth said, with a lazy grin. "I like to get right to the good stuff."

"Breakfast." Erroh tilted his head. "No, lunch. No, breakfast. I can't decide."

"How is this supposed to help us get to know each other better?" Zain asked.

"Just answer the question," I said.

He shrugged. "I don't really have a favorite."

I sighed and turned to Parin, who had been especially quiet ever since he arrived. "And you?"

He gave me a warm smile. "Supper. I like salty foods, and the more pepper the better."

Erroh made a gagging sound. "Parin is obsessed with pepper. He puts it on everything. I'll never forget when Daka and I were sick and Mom and Dad were out, so Parin made us some soup. He put so much pepper in it we nearly gagged."

"Pepper soup!" I laughed. "I remember that."

"Oh," Erroh said, his face falling. "Of course you do."

"My favorite is supper too," I said quickly. "Followed by dessert." Silence hit the table as we all continued eating. I wracked my brain for another question. "Favorite animal?"

"Owl," Erroh said.

"I've always been partial to dolphins," Carth said.

Zain waved a hand. "These questions are silly. We already know everything about each other."

"Not everything," I muttered, but I had to admit it did feel silly asking these questions.

"No? What's the next one—favorite childhood memory?" Zain snorted. "Most of our memories feature each other, I bet."

I leaned forward. "Well, what is your favorite childhood memory?"

Zain looked at me with his intense blue eyes. "The four of us—you, me, Carth, and Erroh—sneaked away one afternoon and headed into the woods. I'm sure it was your idea, Sora."

"It always was," Erroh muttered.

"Shush." I threw a bread roll at him.

"We found that one large, gnarled tree, and Carth challenged us to get to the top first. I was determined to win, but I fell and broke my ankle." Zain paused and something smoldered in his eyes. "You climbed down and healed it."

I remembered the moment. We were young then, but I was right at the age when I was beginning to realize they were boys and I was a girl and that meant something. I turned to Parin, who had gone quiet again. "And then Parin came and found us."

Carth chuckled. "Yes, if I remember correctly, he made us all go back inside."

Parin ducked his head. "I was simply trying to keep you out of trouble."

"That's your favorite memory?" Erroh asked. "Getting injured?"

"I think he probably enjoyed the healing part the most," Carth said with a wry grin.

"I enjoyed being with my friends," Zain snapped.

"I love that memory too," I said. "The best times were when we were all together." Zain has grown up in the Fire Temple or the nearby town of Sparkport, while Carth spent much of his time at his parents' estates in the Air Realm. All my favorite memories were when they came to visit Soulspire with their families.

"Exactly my point," Zain said. "You already know us, better than anyone."

It was hard to argue with that. I did know them, through and through, and there was no way to force the change in mindset from friends to lovers. Only time and togetherness would do that.

I knew Mom said not to rush, but frankly I was already tired of being patient. I wanted to bond with my mates and to gain my elemental powers and my dragon form. Especially if the Death Goddess was rising again.

I set down my fork and looked at the men one by one, even Parin, though the fact that he was one of my mates still hadn't fully sunk in. "We should leave for the Air Temple tomorrow morning."

"I agree," Erroh quickly said.

"Of course you agree," Carth said with a snicker. "But

the sooner we head to the Air Temple, the sooner we can go to the others too."

Zain looked as though he was about to speak, when we heard shouting outside and the sound of running footsteps. We all exchanged a worried glance and shot to our feet, then headed out the door to see what the commotion was about.

The guards were all heading outside toward the front gates, where a large number of soldiers crowded together. Erroh pulled a female guard aside at the door, and asked, "What is this about?"

"They caught the criminal Varek trying to enter the palace!" she said.

My stomach dropped. Varek was the most notorious criminal in Soulspire, leader of a gang called the Quick-blades. He was incredibly mysterious, and although the guard in Soulspire had been trying to capture him for years, he'd always eluded them. I'd never seen him before, only vague sketches from the few witnesses of his criminal activities. Witnesses who usually went missing later. Why was he here?

My mates and I pushed through the crowd to where the soldiers surrounded a tall man with long, black hair and muscular arms covered in tattoos. As soon as I laid eyes on him I jerked to a halt, my heart lurching.

He was the man in my dreams.

Jasin moved forward and leveled a sword at Varek's throat. "Explain your presence here quickly, before we slap you in chains and drag you to our prison."

Varek appeared unphased by this, and way too calm considering dozens of soldiers surrounded him. "I'm here to speak with *her*."

His head turned and when his eyes landed on me I sucked in a sharp breath. As our gazes met, I felt that spark, that connection, that *something* I had with the other men too.

There was no denying it. Varek was my fifth mate.

CHAPTER SIX

I pushed my way through the crowd toward Varek, vaguely aware of my other mates following behind me. Everyone's eyes were on me, until large silvery dragon wings blocked out the moonlight. People scrambled out of the way as my mother landed with a heavy thud, then bared her fangs at Varek.

"What business do you have with my daughter?" Kira roared.

Varek stared back at the dragon without fear, and then bowed, but not out of respect. He made it seem flippant or cocky somehow. "The Death Goddess sends her regards."

Mom let out a roar that would have most men quaking in their boots, but Varek just crossed his arms. Unbelievable.

As I moved beside my mother, my other fathers showed up too. They weren't in their dragon forms, but they were just as intimidating. "Explain yourself," Slade demanded.

Varek's eyes landed on me again. "The Dragon Goddess has named me her champion, and she demands Sora take me as her fifth mate."

A chorus of gasps went up from the soldiers and other onlookers, making me wish we'd gone somewhere private for this conversation.

"Impossible!" Auric said. "The Ascendant has only ever had four mates."

Varek lifted his shoulder in a casual shrug. "Not anymore."

"This is preposterous," Parin said behind me. "Send the man away."

"No," I finally said, my voice ringing out through the courtyard. "He speaks the truth. I've had dreams of him."

"What?" Erroh asked.

Mom shifted and shimmered back into her human form, her brow furrowed. "He is the one from your dreams?"

I nodded, swallowing hard. This dark, deadly, dangerous man was one of my mates. There was no escaping it, no matter how much I wanted to resist the idea. Yet as much as it horrified me, I was drawn to him too. I couldn't look away from his skull tattoos, or the wicked gleam in his eye, or the sensual curl of his lips.

"Prove it," Zain said, and Carth nodded in agreement.

"I don't think you'd like to see my powers in action," Varek said, his voice dripping with threat. "But perhaps a small demonstration is in order."

He bent down and ran his fingers through the grass, and

a wave of death and decay spread out around him, instantly turning it brown and dry. The entire crowd gasped, and the hollowness inside me grew. There was no denying it now. The Death Goddess had given him her magic.

"You don't need him to gain your elemental powers or your dragon form," Reven told me. "You could refuse him."

Varek let out a cruel laugh. "If you refuse, the Death Goddess is prepared to unleash the Realm of the Dead upon the living."

"She wouldn't dare," Mom said.

"She would. She has been denied respect for far too long. Every other God has a Dragon, and she demands one as well."

Hushed mutters and whispers rippled among the crowd, until Jasin called out, "Silence!"

I stepped closer to Varek and faced him, keenly aware of the eyes upon us. "Do you even want to be my mate?"

"I'll serve the Goddess however she requires." His dark gaze turned hungry as it slowly roamed down my body. "Though I can't say it will be a hardship to mate with a princess."

"I'm not a princess," I snapped.

His only response was a harsh laugh. I hated him already, even as the look he gave me sent desire racing through my veins. It wasn't fair—the mating bond made me want him, no matter how awful he was.

"You have a week to accept this, or there will be a war between the living and the dead," Varek said. "Find me at the Lone Wolf Pub in the north end of Soulspire with your answer."

He turned on his heels and began to walk out the gate, but Jasin and Reven raised their swords. "Halt!" Jasin shouted.

Varek laughed. "What are you going to arrest me for? Coming to see my mate? I think not."

No one made a move against him, because he was right. No one would defy the Gods like that. As we all watched, he strolled out of the gate and disappeared into the night.

"I'll follow him," Reven said, before he slipped into the shadows. Having a former assassin as your father had its perks. Or it was going to make everything worse. I couldn't be sure yet.

"Leave us," Jasin commanded, and the guards departed and the crowd reluctantly dispersed.

As soon as they were gone, Mother rushed toward me and pulled me into her arms. I was too horrified and shocked to do anything but let her hold me.

"You're certain he's the one from your dreams?" Mom whispered with her head against mine.

I lifted my head away and nodded. "Yes. I'm sure of it."

"That doesn't mean you have to accept him," Kira said. "We will deal with the Death Goddess. We've done it before."

"I appreciate that, but we can't have a war against the dead," I said.

"I think you need to tell us about these dreams you've been having," Carth said.

I turned to face my mates, who did not look happy—not at all. Erroh was scowling, Parin had his arms crossed, Zain's jaw was clenched, and Carth's usual flirty smile was replaced with a frown.

"I've been having dreams of only one man every night—a man I'd never met until now. At first, I thought he was my Earth mate, but then Parin came and set that to rest."

"You never dreamed of us?" Zain asked.

"No, only of him. I can't deny it—he is my mate, just like the four of you are."

"It's completely out of the question," Jasin, said. "He's the most wanted criminal in Soulspire. The Silver Guard has been trying to dig up something concrete on that man and the Quickblades for years. Every time we get something, there never proves to be enough evidence to charge him, and no one will speak up against him. He cannot be your mate."

"Besides, *we* are your mates," Parin said with a note of finality in his voice. "There are always four, and four alone."

"Not anymore." I sighed. "Believe me, I don't like this any more than you do."

Erroh took my hand. "I'll support whatever you decide, but my vote is to throw him in the dungeon."

I pushed at his shoulder. "That's obviously not an option."

Slade met my eyes, his face filled with fatherly disapproval. "He's a villain, Sora. A criminal."

"Yes, but he seems to be telling the truth," Auric said. "And I don't see the other Gods stepping in to stop the Death Goddess in this matter."

"This is going to be a disaster," Carth muttered.

"Agreed," Zain said. "But we're with you Sora, whatever you decide."

I turned away, my head spinning. Whatever I decided wouldn't just affect me, but my other mates too—and possibly the entire world. We were meant to be guardians, protectors, mediators...could a champion of Death serve those roles too?

"I need to think on this some more," I said with a sigh. "I'll make a decision tomorrow."

Mom nodded. "Only you know the dreams and what they mean. If this is what you must do, so be it. If not, we will stand beside you against the Death Goddess."

I gave her a weak smile. "Thanks. I have a feeling I'll need your help either way."

Mom would support me no matter my decision, and could help me figure out how to navigate being mated to such a man. But my four fathers were another story. They were likely to band together and try to force Varek to leave the city. Or arrest him.

Or kill him.

I went back to my room alone and then paced back and forth

as I went over what happened. It was too early to sleep, and my mind was too restless for that anyway. I had to figure out what to do about Varek or the anxiety would eat me up inside.

I couldn't refuse him. Somehow I knew that deep in my core. Not only because unleashing the dead upon the world was a horrible idea that would sacrifice many lives, but because when I looked at Varek I felt...something. The same connection I had with my other mates, even though I'd never met him before. I didn't want to feel it, but I did.

He was one of my mates and I had to accept that, no matter how much I disliked it.

But accepting it wouldn't make things easier. My other mates I had feelings for, and I knew they cared for me. I could envision sharing many years with them by my side, and knew that love would grow between us. Varek, on the other hand, I could only feel apprehension about. We had no love for each other. Could I ever grow to love the champion of Death? Would he care for me in return?

Pacing back and forth in my bedroom would do nothing to answer these questions. It was time to take action. I hadn't really gotten a chance to speak with Varek because I'd been surrounded by my mates, my parents, and an entire audience of guards and palace staff. I needed to talk to him alone. Tomorrow I planned to go to the Air Temple, and I didn't want to put that off unless I had to. Which meant facing Varek tonight.

I changed from my evening dress into my fighting

leathers, strapped on all of my throwing knives, and put my wild curls up in a high bun, out of my way. Then I donned my black cloak and pulled the hood over my head, before grabbing my sword.

Once I was ready, I opened the large window by my desk and climbed onto the tree, then slipped down into the darkness. Reven had taught me everything about stealth, and I used those skills now to easily maneuver around the patrolling guards and head outside the palace grounds. I was allowed to leave the palace by myself whenever I wanted, since who would dare attack me? But in this matter, I wished to be discreet. I didn't want anyone to ask me questions or try to stop me. Or worse, get my fathers or my mates. They'd all want to send someone with me for protection, and I needed to do this on my own.

Our palace resided inside the great city of Soulspire, located at the center of the four Realms—one each for Fire, Earth, Air, and Water. Soulspire was neutral and not part of any one of them, ruled completely by the Dragons and the Silver Guard. The palace loomed over the city with its shining arches and tall tower in the center, where my parents lived. They told me that in their day the palace had been dark, run-down, and imposing, but now it gleamed like a beacon of peace and stability that all residents of Soulspire could look upon.

I made my way through the dark streets under the faint moonlight, past taverns and cafes bustling with people. Drunken couples stumbled by me, but no one gave me a second glance as I searched for the place Varek had mentioned. I passed a bar filled entirely with elementals, and nearly collided with a water elemental as it came out of the place. Luckily I moved away from its giant watery body in time before I got soaked. It mumbled that I should be more careful in the elemental language, probably assuming I wouldn't understand. Few humans did, but I'd learned it from Auric as a child.

Finally I turned onto a dimly lit street and saw an image of a wolf on a tavern sign. As I got closer, I made out the name *Lone Wolf Pub* above the door. The windows were darkened so I couldn't see anything inside. No music drifted from the black door. No one stumbled out drunk and laughing. Was the place empty? Or closed?

I wiped my damp palms on my trousers, then felt annoyed at myself. I was the daughter of Dragons. Varek was my mate. I had no reason to be nervous.

I opened the door and stepped inside.

CHAPTER SEVEN

The inside of the bar was only lit by a few candles around the room, illuminating dark wooden tables and chairs, plus a few booths with red leather in the back. A large man with a long moustache wiped down the bar from behind the counter while giving me an unfriendly look. The few patrons inside all had a rough edge to them—tattoos, muscles, scowls—and glared at me for daring to enter their pub. Not a friendly crowd.

"I see the princess has come to play," a female voice said to my side.

I turned toward the sound, where a striking woman with long black hair and gray eyes sat in the corner with her legs crossed, revealing thigh-high boots. Her sneer didn't do anything to make me feel like I should stick around another minute.

My fists clenched at the word princess, but I stopped myself from responding. "I'm looking for Varek."

"Of course you are." She rose to her feet and I spotted a large dagger at her waist. "Follow me."

She took me to a door beside the counter, past the scowling bartender, and led me down a dark hallway. We passed two doorways, only one of which was open. As I peered inside, I was shocked to see an enormous room, which must have been built into the hill behind the bar. This place didn't look this big from the outside.

Dozens of people stood inside in a circle, surrounding two huge, sweaty, shirtless men who circled each other while everyone else cheered. One of their fists flew toward the other, but I didn't see the blow land before the door slammed shut.

"That's not for you," the woman said.

"Was that an underground fight club?" I asked, unable to hide the shock in my voice. Such a thing was forbidden by the Silver Guard. Then again, Varek was a known criminal, so I shouldn't have been surprised.

She shrugged and headed around the corner. "Didn't see anything like that."

"Of course not," I muttered.

She stopped at another door and knocked sharply, then waited for the deep, "Come in," on the other side before she opened it.

Varek was inside, sitting behind a large black desk. He

looked up and met my eyes, and that little spark between us made me suck in a sharp breath. Why did the man have to be so damn handsome?

"Oh." Varek looked down at the open notebook on his desk. "It's you."

"That's the welcome I get?" I asked, my blood boiling.

"Better than I got earlier." His eyes shifted to the other woman. "Thank you, Wrill."

Wrill gave him a quick nod, then stepped out and shut the door behind her, after throwing me another sneer.

"She seems lovely," I said.

"She's my sister."

"That explains it then."

He slammed his notebook shut. "You're bold to come walking through the front door of my pub. I thought you'd be a bit more discreet, princess."

"I'm not a princess, and why should I be discreet? If I take you as a mate, everyone in the four Realms will know."

He steepled his long fingers. "I will admit, I'm surprised you came to me so quickly. I thought you'd debate and dawdle for a few days, before finally realizing this is inevitable."

I huffed. "I don't dawdle."

A slow grin spread across his face. "I do like a woman of action."

Something about the way he said it made me flush. What was it about this man that had me so out of sorts? I steeled myself and said, "I've decided to take you as my mate."

"Obviously."

His arrogance only enraged me further. "On one condition."

He arched a dark eyebrow. "Oh?"

"You have to give up your criminal lifestyle."

He tilted his head back and let out a laugh that sounded a lot like a roar. Then he cut it off short and asked, "Anything else?"

"You'll need to move into the palace, of course."

He waved a dismissive hand. "Thanks for the offer, but I'll pass."

"Excuse me? If you are to be my mate, you'll have to give up..." I gestured vaguely to the room around me. "All this and join me at the palace."

"No, I really don't."

My jaw dropped, even though I wanted to remain cool and collected. Who would turn down living at the palace and becoming a Dragon? "What other choice do you have?"

He stood, giving me a good view of his strong arms covered in black ink. "I'll be your mate, don't you fear, but I'm not giving anything up. I'll remain here in the city, while you stay in the palace with your other men."

"Do you even want to be my mate?" I asked, completely flabbergasted.

His eyes narrowed. "The Death Goddess chose me and I will serve her however she commands."

"And she commanded you to be my mate, with everything that involves!" Gods, why was he so damn frustrating?

"Was that all you came for?" He picked up the notebook on his desk and put it on a bookshelf behind him, then turned back to me. "I was hoping you wanted to sample the goods."

"What? No! Why would you possibly think that?"

"Too bad. I made the bed and everything." His eyes moved to something behind me, and I followed his gaze to a bed large enough for two. When I'd entered the room, I'd had nothing but eyes for him, and now I saw that this office also served as a bedchamber, probably a temporary one.

I was suddenly extremely aware that I was alone in a room with a criminal and a bed. I'd eventually need to have sex with this man, but he would not be my first. I'd kill him before that happened, Death Goddess be damned. I was more than capable of doing that.

"Go back to your palace." He walked around the desk and slowly approached me. I held my ground, unwilling to give him an inch. "You may be the princess of this city, but I'm the king. One day, you'll bow to me too."

"Never."

He was so close now I could smell him. Leather, mixed with something faint and spicy. Something dangerous. Our eyes were locked together, and I found myself breathing faster, my heart pounding. Even worse, his body called to mine. Heat from his chest ran across my breasts, making my nipples harden under my leather top. I wanted him to touch me, while at the same time I wanted to push him away.

His head tilted down and he seemed to breathe me in, and for a second I thought he would press his lips to mine. I held my breath, waiting to see what he would do. But then he stepped back and turned away.

"Run home, little princess, before your watchdogs realize you're slumming it here with us criminals."

Unbelievable. "If you won't come to the palace, I don't see how we can be mates."

"I'm sure we'll figure something out." He sat behind his desk again and leaned back in his chair, crossing his tattooed arms behind his head. "Come back when you're ready to head to the Death Temple for our bonding."

I grit my teeth, but I had nothing more to say to this awful man. I turned and stomped toward the door, ready to be far away from him.

As soon I touched the knob, he said, "Wait."

I turned back and saw him stalking toward me, his long black hair flowing behind him, making my breath catch. "Yes?"

He brushed past me and opened the door. "I'll show you out the back."

I rolled my eyes and followed him down the hallway. "Why, don't want me to see more of your illegal activities?"

"I think you've seen enough for one night."

He opened a door at the far end and a cool rush of outdoor air flew inside, along with the sound of many voices.

As I started forward, Varek threw a large, inked arm in front of me. "Stop."

"What is it?" I asked.

"Something you should stay away from."

"Why?" I craned my head, trying to see out. "What's happening out there?"

I pushed past him and he sighed and let me go. I stepped outside and saw a large crowd gathered around a person in a featureless black mask standing on a crate beside a statue of my mother in dragon form. Other people in gray masks stood around in support, staring out at the people gathered there.

The person on the crate raised a fist. "For too long, humans have been powerless, while the elementals and the Dragons use their magic to control the world. We all know this peace with the elementals won't last. There are reports every day of elementals and shades attacking human settlements in the outer reaches, and where are the Dragons? In their lofty tower, lording over us. We can't rely on them to protect us any longer. They've sided with the enemy. We need to defend ourselves and rise up against the oppressors. It's time to put humans first again!"

My jaw dropped as I stared at the leader, but then Varek grabbed my hood and yanked it down over my head. "It would be best if you weren't seen."

"Why? Trying to protect me from them?" I hadn't expected that from him.

He gave me a dark glare. "I don't want to lose my mate before claiming her."

I shook my head at him and moved forward, trying to get a better look. I'd never heard this kind of talk before. The Dragons were the protectors of the Four Realms. Their while purpose was to keep humans safe. Did these people truly believe they were doing such a bad job of it?

"We are the Unseen, but we will not be ignored any longer!" The speaker on the crate spread their arms, and flames burst forth from their fingertips. I gasped and actually stumbled back. That wasn't possible. I could count on one hand the number of people with fire magic, and none of them would be saying something like this. For a second I wondered if this was some kind of prank and it was Zain up there, or my father, but that didn't make any sense.

Fists went up in the air with the chant, "Humans first!" I gazed around, shocked by the vehemence in their voices and the anger on their faces, as much as the leader's fire display. Varek grabbed my arm as the crowd started throwing bottles and rocks at the statue of Kira. He had to drag me out of there, and I was too stunned and horrified to do anything but go along with him.

"That was a trick, right? That person didn't really use magic?" I asked, as we turned a corner and went out of view of the crowd. I could still hear them in the distance, along with the sound of another bottle smashing. I cringed as I stumbled forward. "Do they really believe all that?"

Varek didn't answer me, but kept leading me down

alleys and dark streets I'd never visited before, until the gates of the palace came into view. Only then did he stop.

He released the grip on my arm, and I absently rubbed the spot where his hand had been. I looked up at him, realizing that he'd gotten me out of a dangerous situation and escorted me home. Maybe he wasn't as bad as I'd thought.

"You know where to find me," he said. "Try to be a little less obvious next time."

My eyes narrowed. "I don't need to hide or sneak around. I'm the Ascendant."

His laugh mocked me. "Did you learn nothing from that rally? The streets of Soulspire are no longer safe for you."

I could only gape at him as he slipped back into the shadows and left me alone with my dark thoughts.

The guards didn't react as I walked through the gates. Nor did the guards at the door, or the two I passed going up the stairs to my wing of the palace.

When I walked into my chambers, though, my mates blinked several times at me. "Where have you been?" Erroh asked. "We thought you were in bed."

They sat around the living area, drinking what looked like ale. I shrugged off my cloak. "I couldn't sleep, so I went to talk to Varek."

"What?" Zain asked. "Why would you do that alone?"

I strode forward and took Erroh's drink from his hand, gulping it down. I needed it, after what I'd just been through. "To take him as my mate, of course."

"I thought you were going to make your decision in the morning," Parin said.

"I didn't want to delay our trip to the Air Temple, and besides, there was no real decision to make. I have to take him as my mate. Unleashing the Death Goddess upon the world is not an option."

"But—" Erroh started.

I held up a hand. "It's not just that. I feel it. The mate-bond. Just like I feel it with all of you. There's no denying the Gods' will. I have to do this."

The men glanced at each other with wary expressions, before Carth finally cracked a grin and said, "Well, the more the merrier, in my opinion. I'm just eager to get started."

"Is Varek even willing to be your mate?" Zain asked.

"He's going to be difficult," I said with a sigh. "He doesn't want to leave the Quickblades or move into the palace. But there's something else I need to tell you."

"What is it?" Parin asked.

"When I left Varek's pub, I encountered a crowd with all these people wearing gray masks that covered their entire faces. Their leader stood on a crate and gave a speech about how humans were oppressed by the elementals and the Dragons and it was time to put humans first again."

"Oh." Erroh nodded his head. "I've heard of them. The Unseen. They used to be a small human rights group, very anti-elemental, but otherwise harmless. They've recently been growing in numbers in Soulspire though and have become something more like a cult, so Jasin's had some of the Silver Guard keeping an eye on them."

"I didn't see any Silver Guard tonight when they were throwing things at the statue of my mother," I said, clenching my fists at the memory.

"They did that?" Zain asked.

"Yes, and there's more too." I sank into the only empty chair. The room had been designed to hold five of us comfortably. We'd have to rethink it if Varek joined us. "I saw the leader controlling fire."

Zain shook his head. "Not possible. Only Kira, Jasin, and I can control fire, along with the High Priestess of the Fire Temple. I strongly doubt any of them would be doing such a thing."

"He's right," Parin said. "Humans have never been able to control the elements. The Gods do not favor them that way."

"It could've been a trick," Erroh suggested. "They could've contrived something to make the crowd think they had magic to get a reaction from them."

"That's what I thought too, but it seemed so...real," I said.

"It can't be real." Zain reached over and stroked my arm. "I'm sure the rally was upsetting to witness, but you must put it from your mind and focus on what is important—bonding with us so that you can become a Dragon."

"He's right," Carth said. "Tomorrow you'll start going to the temples and we'll put all this from your mind."

I nodded slowly. Between Varek and the demonstration, my stomach was all twisted up in knots. We had to leave first thing in the morning, and me brooding over Varek or the human wielding fire wouldn't help me bond with my mates.

I said good night to my men and retreated to my bed alone, but no matter how I tried, I couldn't get what I'd seen off my mind. Sleep was a long time coming.

CHAPTER EIGHT

After some debate, we decided it would be faster and easier if only Erroh and I went to the Air Temple while everyone else stayed behind. There was nothing in the books that said all my mates had to be there for the bonding, after all. Additionally, the Air Temple was to the east, while the Water Temple—our next destination—was to the west, so we'd have to come back to Soulspire anyway. My other mates weren't thrilled about it, but the journey would take Auric, the fastest of the Dragons, a full day of flying as it was. He'd volunteered to take me, as the Air Dragon, and none of my other fathers had argued. Slade seemed relieved he wouldn't have to go, actually.

Just after dawn, we stood out in the courtyard with Auric already in his dragon form, his golden scales gleaming bright under the morning sunlight. I held up a hand to cover a yawn, wishing I'd managed more sleep last night. Or any night since my Ascension.

I was quickly saying goodbye to my other parents and my mates, while Erroh said farewell to his own family. Cadock and Faya took turns hugging him, then stepped back beside Parin.

Faya smiled at them both. "It's so incredible and... surprising that the Gods chose each of you for Sora's mates."

"Yes, it was a shock when we were both chosen." Parin cleared his throat and turned to his brother. "Good luck at the Air Temple."

"I'm not sure we need luck, but thanks," Erroh said, with a slight frown.

"We're very proud of you two," Cadock said, clasping a hand on both of his sons' shoulders. Although Parin was technically his adopted son, Cadock had never treated him any differently from his other children.

I turned away from them and hugged Carth next. "Enjoy yourself," he whispered, then pressed a kiss to my neck.

"Are you sure we can't come with you?" Zain asked. "Although I grew up in the Fire Temple, I've never visited the others."

Kira shook her head. "I'm sorry, but I need Sora's other fathers' help. We received reports this morning that the elementals on Divine Isle are demanding more land in the four Realms, and we need to travel there to speak with them before any fighting breaks out. Especially with the rumors of elementals going missing fueling their anger."

"Besides, none of us want to be there when *it* happens," Jasin said, wrinkling his nose.

Reven rolled his eyes. "Sora's a grown woman now. We knew this would happen."

"Doesn't mean we have to like it," Slade muttered.

"She'll be fine," Mom said, shaking her head with an amused smile.

I wanted nothing more than to escape this awkward moment where everyone was talking about me having sex without actually saying it out loud. Thank the Gods all of my parents weren't coming. Having one at the temple would be bad enough.

"Let's go," I said, taking Erroh's hand and practically dragging him toward Auric. We climbed onto my father's hard, scaly back, and then waved at everyone and shouted our goodbyes, as Auric lifted up into the air with a flap of his great golden wings.

Flying was my favorite thing in the world. My fathers always loved taking me for rides, soaring high above the city with the sunshine soaking into our skin. As a kid, they took me all over the four Realms with them, even to the elementals' Divine Isle, and I was completely comfortable riding on a dragon for long hours. But whereas I grew up with dragon-riding as my main form of transportation, Erroh and my other mates had not.

Erroh was probably the only one who had ever ridden a

dragon before, actually. As kids, we'd sometimes gotten a quick ride from one of my dads, but it had been many years since then.

Erroh seemed to remember though. He wrapped his arms around me and let out a loud whoop as we ascended high into the sky and zoomed over Soulspire. His joy was contagious, and I found myself grinning as the wind buffeted my face and tugged at my tied-back hair. His arms squeezed me tight, and I leaned back against him. If it wasn't for the fact that we were sitting on top of Auric, I would've found the experience of finally being able to rest in his arms very alluring.

Since Soulspire was located at the cross point of all four Realms, we entered the Air Realm immediately and soared over forests that changed to rolling hills and then to sharp mountains. We stopped briefly for lunch on a rocky cliff, and while we munched on packed bread, meat, and cheese, Auric told us about what it was like when he traveled to the Air Temple to bond with my mother, from riding on camels to finding the temple destroyed and the priests killed to fighting two of the previous Dragons in the air. I'd heard the story many times before, of course, but Erroh hung onto every word. Then we set off again, flying over the barren desert of Sandstorm Valley while the relentless sun beat down on us.

A few hours later, after the sun had set, the Air Temple came into view—a large sand-colored tower that reached high into the clouds, surrounded by a small lake with palm trees. It was the only thing in sight for miles amid the endless, empty desert. During my parents' rule, the Air Temple had been rebuilt and a new High Priestess had been chosen. I'd been there a few times with my parents, but things were different now that I was coming here with a new purpose.

"Is that where we'll meet the Air God?" Erroh asked, shielding his eyes to peer at the temple's grounds.

"No, it will be on the roof," Auric's dragon voice rumbled.

After we bonded and I gained Erroh's powers, the Air God would come and speak to us. For my parents, they'd answered a few questions and gave some cryptic information, but I had no idea what they would say to me.

Auric landed in front of the Air Temple and kicked up some sand with his wings. High Priestess Blair, a dark-skinned woman in her fifties with gray-streaked black hair, approached us with a kind smile. She wore a loose yellow robe with bare shoulders, while her mates trailed behind her. Like me and my mom, the High Priestesses each got four mates to serve as their priests.

"Welcome Sora," Blair said, clasping my hands in her own. "We are honored to be the first temple in your travels." Then she turned toward Erroh and also took his hands. "And a fond greeting to our next Air Dragon."

"Thank you," Erroh said, as he glanced at the priests watching on. He had to be as overwhelmed as I was, but he was doing a good job of hiding it so far. "I'm very lucky to have been chosen."

"It's good to see you again," Auric said to Blair.

"Always an honor, Air Dragon," she said with a bow.

Auric waved a hand. "You know you don't need to do that. I had enough bowing when I was a prince."

"Of course. Please, come inside," Blair said. "We've prepared everything for your bonding. Would you like a meal or a bath first?"

Although I was quite dusty and hadn't eaten since lunch, I had no desire for either of those things. I'd waited for this moment for years and all I wanted was to get on with it, but I also didn't want to seem too eager in front of my father. "A meal would be lovely, thanks."

Blair and her mates led us into a large dining room, with big windows open to the cool night breeze floating inside. We shared a quick meal that lasted longer than I hoped, during which Blair asked Erroh about himself. I suppose it was important for the High Priestess to get to know her next Dragon, but I couldn't wait to be finished. Judging by the way Erroh's hand moved to my leg under the table and began stroking my thigh, I knew he felt the same.

When dinner finally ended, Auric kissed my forehead and gave me a warm smile. "I'm happy the Air God chose Erroh. He is a good man and I know he will treat you well."

"Me too." Somehow Dad knew exactly what to say to make me feel better about all this.

"You know, I was a virgin too when I came here and—"

I quickly held up a hand and tried not to gag. "Please stop right there."

Dad gave me a goofy grin. "All right. I just want you to know everything will be fine."

He gave me a warm hug, and then shook Erroh's hand, before going with the priests into the library, his favorite place.

Blair led us up a never ending spiral staircase, and even though Erroh and I were both in great shape, by the time we reached the top, we were both out of breath and needed a second to recover. Flying up here would have been so much easier.

It was worth it though once we stepped through the doorway onto the open-air platform at the top of the temple. Most of the clouds had disappeared, and from here all I could see was endless night sky, sparkling stars, and the thin sliver of the crescent moon. Oh, and the large bed waiting for us.

"Please let me know if you need anything else," Blair said, before bowing and then heading back down the stairs.

Erroh met my eyes. "Finally, we're alone."

CHAPTER NINE

I looked down at myself, suddenly nervous. I'd packed a light bag with a change of clothes and a silky tunic that would be more appropriate than my traveling clothes, but hadn't changed into them yet. I'd expected to have more time to prepare somehow.

I sucked in a sharp breath. "I'm dusty."

Erroh chuckled. "I can fix that."

With the sweep of his hand, a breeze swirled around me and sent the dust flying. It also undid my bun, loosening my hair, and we both laughed as my curls went wild.

He moved close and tried to smooth my hair down with a grin. "Sorry! I'm still learning."

I pressed my hands to his cheeks. There was no reason for me to be nervous, not when I was here with my best friend. "You're perfect."

With his hands still tangled in my hair, we moved

together for a kiss. It started out sweet, but quickly turned deeper, as the magnitude of the moment settled upon us. After so many years wishing we could be together but fearing it was impossible, tonight we would finally be bound together as mates.

Erroh broke off the kiss to lead me to the large bed, where he began unlacing his shirt, then shrugged it off as I stared in amazement at his sculpted chest. I'd seem him shirtless before, and it had been like looking upon a dessert I wasn't allowed to eat.

Tonight I could devour him.

I began removing my own shirt as Erroh watched, and his eyes flew straight to my hands as they moved down my chest. The weight of his gaze excited me and made me want to keep going. When my shirt was completely undone, I left it on so it gaped in the front without exposing my breasts.

We both pulled off our boots next, and when I bent down, my breasts spilled out of my shirt. When I rose, the shirt slid off my shoulders to the floor behind me, leaving me exposed. Erroh's sharp breath told me he liked the sight. I'd never been naked in front of a man before, but I wasn't shy either, and the look on Erroh's face encouraged me to keep going.

He put his thumbs in the waistband of his pants and tugged down. I mimicked him, both of us kicking off our trousers simultaneously. And there it was. My first glimpse of the completely naked male form. I'd seen men fighting, sparring, swimming, but never this part of them.

His hard cock pointed at me as if it knew the direction it wanted him to move, and he stepped close, sliding his arms around my waist. I had to touch him too. I couldn't help myself. Lifting my hands, I placed one on his hard chest and the other on his neck as I stared at his lips, willing him to take the lead. His calloused hands slid down my hips while he pressed his lips to mine, and I gasped against him as his tongue pushed into my mouth. My body acted of its own accord, arching toward him, eager for his naked body to press against mine.

"Erroh," I breathed when he stopped kissing me to trail his lips down my neck.

"I'm sure you know this, but I've never done this before. Have you?"

He paused and then looked up at me. "Only a few times. When you made it clear we couldn't be together, I tried to use other women to forget you, but it never helped, not one bit. The only woman I've ever wanted is you."

My cheeks flushed at that, and he pulled me back against him and resumed his exploration of my body with his tongue. I ran my hands down his body, then lost myself for a moment as his lips closed around my nipple. Sensations I'd never experienced before shot through my body, right to my core, and I sensed I was growing wet. His hands on my naked skin only increased my desire, as did the feel of his hard body under my fingertips. Years of looking but not touching had finally ended in this moment, and I couldn't get enough.

Neither could Erroh. He sucked on each of my breasts while stroking my body slowly, then we floated together toward the big bed. He set me down upon it, then spread my legs wide as he hovered over me. I thought it would happen, his cock finally breaching me, but then his head dropped.

He grinned up at me. "I want to make sure you're nice and ready for me so there's no pain. Don't worry, I read all about this in a book."

It was such an Erroh thing to say that I laughed, but the sound quickly died in my throat as his mouth pressed to the aching spot between my legs. Pleasure like I'd never experienced before spread through me as his tongue danced along my folds and his fingers slid inside me, and then he did things that had me moaning so loud, I briefly worried the people in the temple might be able to hear us. I didn't much care though, especially when he sucked on me in a way that caused an orgasm to sweep through me like a tornado.

As my body twitched with warm pleasure, he slowly moved up my body, until he hovered over me. His eyes gazed into mine as his cock brushed against my thigh. "Are you ready?"

"Gods, yes," I managed, reaching up to wrap my arms around his neck.

"I love you, Sora. I always have."

"I love you too."

He captured my lips in a passionate kiss as his hard length slowly pushed inside me. The pressure was intense and I gasped, but then he paused and waited for me to adjust to his size. I had nothing to compare it to, but he felt huge inside me, and I wasn't sure how he would ever fit. But he took his time until he was all the way inside, filling me completely.

"Sora, this is incredible," Erroh said, pressing his face against my shoulder. "I dreamed of this moment for so long, and it's even better than I expected."

I wasn't so sure, until he began to slowly slide in and out of me, and then things quickly turned pleasurable again. Soon my body took over, instinctively knowing how to move in time with his body so that we rocked together, taking us to new heights. I dug my nails into his shoulders as he thrust inside me faster, and all I could do was moan and hold on to him as the pleasure built. He slipped one hand between us and began stroking me in time with his movements, and I threw my head back as another climax took hold of me. He let out a shout as he increased his pace and came at the same time, spilling his seed inside me.

As he did, a huge gust of wind swept around us, then lifted us into the air. Even knowing something about what to expect, it made me gasp and cling harder to Erroh. The air swirled around our entwined bodies and we flew high up among the stars, the cool night breeze kissing our naked skin. Power spread through me like crackling lightning, but Erroh only held me tighter, until we slowly floated back down to the bed.

The wind disappeared as quickly as it started, and Erroh

and I gazed into each other's eyes. "Nothing has ever felt so right as this moment," he said.

I reached up to play with his dark hair. "We're mates now, for all time. Bonded together for the rest of our lives."

"It's about damn time." He grinned and lowered his head for another kiss.

We stayed on the bed like that for some time, just kissing and lazily exploring each other's bodies, before I remembered there was more to this bonding ritual. We reluctantly put our clothes back on, with plans to take them off again soon and return to bed, then made our way to the edge of the platform. Erroh glanced at me and squeezed my hand, with eager eyes and a nervous smile. This was where the Air God had appeared to my parents, and we held our breath while we waited for him to arrive.

And we waited.

And we waited.

And the Air God never came.

CHAPTER TEN

We had sex two more times that night, just in case that was the problem, but the Air God still never appeared to give us his blessing. Eventually we slept, tangled in each other's arms and legs, with sated smiles on our faces.

As dawn's bright light woke us, we made love again, just for good measure, but then we grew worried.

"This isn't normal," I said. "Not from everything I've been told. The Air God should have spoken to us."

"Can you use air magic?" Erroh asked.

"I don't know." I reached out a hand toward the bed, and to my surprise, the sheets began to moved a little. "Yes, I think so!"

"That's good. The bonding worked then."

"Can you turn into a dragon?"

"I'm not really sure how, but I can try." Erroh's brows

furrowed in concentration, but then golden scales began to slide across his skin. His body grew larger, shifting and changing, until he grew wings and a long tail, along with sharp fangs and talons. He let out a roar and stomped his feet, swishing his tail around, and then gave me what I think was a toothy grin. "That was incredible!"

I laughed and rested a hand on his golden snout. "I guess the Air God isn't coming, but he gave us both his blessing anyway. I'll have to ask Auric what he thinks on our way home."

"Hopefully the Air God doesn't regret his choice," Erroh said, in his rasping dragon voice.

"Of course he doesn't. If he did, you wouldn't be a dragon right now. Let me see your wings." He spread them wide, and I walked around him and stroked the scales. "Very nice. I can't wait to ride you."

He snorted. "I thought you just did that."

I rolled my eyes. "You'll probably need to practice flying, but maybe not. Auric got the hang of it instantly, while Jasin and Slade needed more practice. Either way, soon I'll be able to fly beside you."

"Get on," he said. "I want to see what it feels like."

"I'm naked!"

"After what we just did, I don't think that matters."

With a laugh, I climbed up and settled myself on his back, his hard scales pressing into my core. He walked across the platform, spreading his wings, and I enjoyed the feel of his muscles moving under my legs and excitable areas. Then

I climbed off, and he shifted back into his human form. I could tell he wanted to try flying, but probably not from this great height.

Once we dressed, we headed back down the tower, where we met my dad outside the library. "How did it go?" he asked.

Erroh and I exchanged a worried glance. "Um..." I started.

Auric's face fell. "Oh no. Was it awkward? I know first times can be difficult but—"

"No! It's not that!" I said, my face turning red.

Erroh rubbed the back of his neck. "All of that was fine. Really good actually."

I had to quickly get us back on track before this became more awkward. "The Air God never visited us."

Auric's jaw dropped. "What?"

We quickly explained what happened, minus all the naughty parts, and confirmed the bonding worked. Dad said he'd never read about anything like that occurring before. We asked Blair and the priests about it, but they were just as surprised as we were, although they'd also not spoken to the God for some time either. That was pretty normal though— they often only appeared to choose a new High Priestess and after the Ascension bonding.

After a quick breakfast we set off for Soulspire, with Auric promising to show Erroh how to fly later and to give me some rudimentary air magic lessons. As we flew, it was hard not to feel disappointment though. I'd expected to meet a God, and he'd never arrived. Was I not worthy of his time? Or did this have something to do with the Death Goddess and my fifth mate? Hopefully once I bonded with Carth at the Water Temple we'd gain more insight into the matter.

When we arrived home that night I hoped to be able to speak with my mother, but she and my other dads had already left for Divine Isle to meet with the elementals, and there was a note requesting Auric join them the next day. My other mates grilled Erroh for details, but I was exhausted and wanted nothing more than to collapse in my bed.

Finally, I got a good night's sleep.

In the morning, I was excited to get to work. When I got outside, I found Auric and Erroh already in a nearby field in their dragon forms, and I watched from afar as my father taught my mate how to fly up into the air. Erroh caught on quickly, like he was born to be a dragon, and I laughed as he started doing flips in the sky. I laughed even harder when he crashed right into Auric, making them both fall a little, until their wings caught them.

They shifted back to human form as I approached. "That was fun to watch," I said.

"I got a little carried away there," Erroh said. "Sorry."

"It's fine." Auric smiled at us both. "I still remember

how thrilling it was to be a dragon at first. Sora, I'd hoped to begin your air training today, but unfortunately Kira wishes me to visit Divine Isle to speak with the elementals. I'm sure Erroh can give you some tips though, and I can help you both some more when I return."

"I'd like that." I said, giving him a hug.

Soon he was flying across the sky as a dragon again, and Erroh started showing me a few of the things Auric had taught him. While we were training, my other mates joined us to practice their own magic. It was so easy being around them, joking and laughing as we'd done our entire lives, with the exception of Parin. He stood a little apart from us, solemn and stiff, like he wasn't sure he belonged there. I wasn't entirely sure either, although my pulse quickened when I looked at his handsome face.

Afterward, we all headed into the city to share a drink at a pub, although not Varek's one, of course. We stayed on the other side of the city entirely, though I distantly wondered if I should have invited him. No, he'd been clear he wanted nothing to do with this part of being my mate.

"To Erroh and Sora!" Carth said, as he raised his tankard of ale with a wink. "And to getting that over with, so we can head to the Water Temple tomorrow!"

We all raised our glasses and laughed, before chugging our ale down. Then Erroh wrapped an arm around my shoulders. "We had a pretty incredible night. Are you sure you want to follow that?"

Carth smirked. "I'm sure I can manage to top whatever you did."

Parin held up a hand, his face serious. "Wait. Have you noticed it's cleared out in here?"

I set down my ale and glanced around the tavern. Parin was right—when we'd entered, the place had been packed, but now only a few people in hoods sat at various spots around the room. The bartender and serving staff were gone too.

Then the people in hoods all stood and turned toward us, wearing those same blank gray masks as the protestors the other night.

I hastily pushed my chair back and stood. "We have company."

There were about twelve of them, and they didn't have any weapons. Then again, we'd left most of ours behind too. But we had magic.

"We are the Unseen, and we reject the rule of the Dragons," one of them said, wearing a black mask. Then she—I think it was a she, anyway—opened her hand and shot a ball of fire at us. We jumped out of the way, hitting the dirty, sticky floor as the flames engulfed the table where we'd been sitting. I could only gape at it, and at the person who must be their leader.

"Believe me now?" I asked the guys, as we all scrambled to our feet and summoned our elemental powers. Carth dumped a bucketful of water on the table, dousing the flames, just as the woman sent another burst of fire at us.

This time Zain managed to gain control of it and throw it back at her, but then one of the other masked people used water to stop it.

That meant more of them had powers. Maybe *all* of them. How?

I didn't have time to find out, not when the elemental attacks came quickly. Floorboards ripped up and flew toward us in sharp, pointed stakes. Chairs and tables were blown into us, along with tankards and other glasses. Shards of ice shot toward us, along with balls of fire. The attack came from all sides, and we were totally surrounded and outnumbered.

"Shift into a dragon!" Zain called to Erroh, as he melted a shard of ice midair.

Erroh used his air magic to toss a chair out of the way. "I can't—there's not enough room in here!"

I tried to use my air magic to blast someone back, but I only made a light breeze. Damn, I needed more practice. Instead, I kicked one of the Unseen in the chest, then knocked them out with a quick move Reven taught me. One down. Many to go.

It was a good reminder that I didn't need elemental magic or weapons to take people down. I'd been trained by the best, after all. I moved through the pub room, using my combat and parkour skills to avoid attacks and knock the attackers down, while my mates handled the magic flying all around us.

Suddenly the tavern door burst open, and Varek stood in

the doorway. He grabbed the nearest cultist by the throat and the life drained out of the screaming man, turning his skin black.

"Leave this place, or death will find you too," his voice boomed out, making everyone pause. I couldn't help but stare at him too. Darkness surrounded Varek like a cloak, and he looked absolutely terrifying.

And devastatingly handsome.

He wore a shirt that showed off his muscular, inked arms, and with his hands clenched he stalked forward toward another cultist. The masked person stepped back quickly, but they were too slow, and Varek grabbed them next. As death took the cultist, the other Unseen all stumbled and tripped and forced their way out of the building. By the time the cultist's body hit the ground, the tavern was empty of everyone except us, along with the people we'd already taken down.

Varek ripped the mask off the dead cultist and tossed it aside, then shook his head in disgust.

"What did you do?" I asked. "You killed those people!"

"I'm not the only one." He gestured at some other cultists we'd taken out in the battle.

I set my hands on my hips. "That was self-defense. And many of them are unconscious, not dead. You didn't have to kill them!"

"I was defending you," he snapped. "I'm the champion of Death. This is my way."

"I didn't need defending!"

"How did you know we were here?" Parin asked, as he stepped over a broken chair to approach us.

"I heard there would be an attack from my informants." Varek shot me an arrogant look. "Aren't you glad I have a criminal organization now?"

"We had it under control," I snapped.

"I'm not so sure about that." Erroh glanced down at his arm and winced at the burn there.

"You were right about the human with fire powers," Zain said. "We shouldn't have dismissed your concerns. It was just hard to believe without seeing it with my own eyes."

"And they had not only fire, but all the elements," Parin added.

"The Unseen are getting elemental magic somehow." I moved across the room and took Erroh's arm in my hands, then let out some of my healing life magic. The burn vanished and the skin repaired itself in seconds. "We need to find out how."

"We *need* to head to the Water Temple," Carth said, his voice serious for once. "We were outnumbered today. We need to finish bonding with Sora so we're all at full strength for the next attack."

I wished my parents were in Soulspire so I could talk to them about what happened tonight. With them gone, it was even more reason to become dragons quickly so we could defend ourselves and the city. Mother had told me not to rush, but what other choice did I have?

I sighed. "We'll leave first thing in the morning, though it might take longer without a ride from one of my dads."

"I'll fly you," Erroh said. "I just need a good night's rest first."

"I'll see what my people can learn about the Unseen and how they're getting magic," Varek said.

I bit my lip, but then forced out, "Thank you."

Varek moved close and looked down at me with smoldering intensity. My breath caught when it seemed as though he might kiss me, and try as I might to ignore the attraction between us, I couldn't. His very presence tugged at me and made me want to step into his arms and embrace his darkness.

"Try not to get killed before our bonding," he growled, and all the desire vanished.

Or so I told myself.

CHAPTER ELEVEN

In the morning, Carth's parents met us outside before our departure. Brin was a nobleman from the Air Realm who'd disobeyed her parents' wishes and married Leni, Slade's younger sister. Since they couldn't have children of their own, they'd adopted Carth and his older sister, who was back at their estates.

Brin stroked Carth's sandy hair with pride and love in her eyes. "We're so proud of you, son. But couldn't you have been chosen by the Air God instead?"

Leni laughed and nudged her wife. "Carth was born in the Water Realm. It's in his very soul, even if we raised him in the Air Realm. Just like my heart will always belong to the Earth Realm."

"I know, I'm only teasing," Brin said. "I think you'll make an excellent Water Dragon."

"Thanks, Moms." Carth gave her a hug, and then did the same with Leni.

"Now you take good care of my niece," Leni said, pinching Carth's cheeks.

"I'll do my best." He winked at me.

Leni gave me a warm hug next. "Do try to keep him in line, dear. I know it won't be easy."

I laughed. Brin and Leni were my favorite relatives by farr. "I'm not sure anyone can do that."

"We have faith in you," Brin said, as she took Leni's hand. "Now get going, I want to see Carth as a dragon already."

With those words, we said our goodbyes and climbed onto Erroh, then took off.

The Water Temple was the second farthest one away from Soulspire, and Erroh had only had a few hours of flying practice. Lucky for us, he was a natural at flying, which was probably normal for an Air Dragon, but he still wasn't used to going long distances. It didn't help that the Water Realm was mostly made up of hundreds of islands, so we couldn't exactly travel the distance by foot either.

I rode Erroh with Carth's arms wrapped around me. This experience was far different than when I rode on my fathers' backs. The feel of the powerful dragon moving under me and Carth's arms around me were powerful aphrodisiacs, and I was eager to get to the temple.

At midday, we stopped in a fishing village for lunch, and were able to board a small boat to give Erroh a few hours to rest. He passed out in the back of the boat with a blanket over his head to shield him from the sun. Then at sunset the boat docked, and we continued flying again until we found another island with an inn to rest in for the night.

We finally reached the island near the Water Temple by the next afternoon. Erroh's taloned feet crashed down on the sand, and he swung his large head around. "Are you sure this is the right place?"

I folded up the map and slid off his back. "Yes, this is it."

Neither one of them had been to the Water Temple before, but I'd visited a few times with my dads. The island we stood on had one lone palm tree and was about the size of my bedroom in the palace. Nothing about it indicated the Water Temple was below. Originally there had been another Water Temple, but after it was destroyed the High Priestess and her mates moved to this secret one. When the danger had passed, they simply decided to stay.

Carth jumped off of Erroh and peered into the water. "It's under there? How will we get down there without drowning?"

"With our magic, of course," I said with a laugh. "Erroh and I can wrap a bubble of air around ourselves, and you can keep the water away from you." Both guys looked skeptical, and I rolled my eyes. "Trust me, I've done it before. Well, I've seen it done, anyway. How hard can it be?"

"I'm not sure I want to find out while at the bottom of the ocean," Erroh said, after shifting to his human form.

"We can practice up here first." I slipped off my shoes,

rolled up my trousers to my knees, and waded into the ocean. The two guys slowly followed me.

It took a lot more practice than we expected, but hours later we were continuing our journey underwater toward the Water Temple. Erroh was back in dragon form, and together we kept a bubble of air around us, keeping us dry and allowing us to breath, while Carth used water to propel us forward. We dove down into the clear blue waters, passing a few fish, and then Erroh paused at the sharp drop into the darker depths. I felt the same hesitation—if our magic failed, we would all drown—but then I stroked his shoulder and said, "We can do this."

He used his wings to dive down into the darkness, and although I expected this, it was still terrifying to be in the middle of the ocean unable to see anything, not knowing which way was up anymore. But then a light came into view, and we began to make out the beautiful, pale building of the Water Temple at the bottom of the ocean.

I directed Erroh on where to land, and we stopped on the ocean floor beside a large dragon sculpture before walking into the large dome of air that surrounded the temple. My skin tingled as we passed through, and then we dropped our air bubble. The Water God protected the temple so it's priests could live there safely.

A small woman with black hair and olive skin emerged from the stone door of the temple, wearing a sea-green robe. Wella was only ten years older than I was and had recently taken over from her mother as High Priestess. Now her stomach was round with her pregnancy, and she waddled out to us with a warm smile. Her four handsome priests followed after her, some of them looking on with concern.

"Welcome!" she said, and then gathered me in a friendly hug. "We weren't sure when to expect you, but we're so happy you're here now."

"Thank you. It looks like we came at a good time." I gestured at her round stomach. "When are you due?"

"Any day now," she said with a laugh. "Don't worry, we've prepared everything for you. Mostly my priests, since they won't let me do anything these days."

I laughed and gestured at my mates. "This is Erroh, my Air Dragon, and Carth, who will be my Water Dragon."

Carth stepped forward and took Wella's hands in his own and gave them a light kiss. "You look radiant. Your husbands are very lucky."

Wella blushed in a cute way. "An honor to meet you. Please come inside."

We followed Wella and her priests into the great temple, walking over shiny sea green tiles through sand-colored rooms. She showed us to our rooms for the evening, where we quickly freshened up, and then we all shared a quick meal together. Wella and I did most of the talking, catching up on how she's been and how her mother is doing in retirement. Then Erroh went to his room to collapse in exhaustion, and Wella led Carth and me to the bonding room.

My heart beat quickened as the door opened. Flickering candlelight revealed a raised platform in the middle of the room with a large bed on it, similar to the one at the Air Temple. However, this platform was surrounded by a pool of knee-deep water, with shiny seashells along the floor. On the other side of the bed there was an entire wall missing, opening the room to the ocean, although the dome of air kept us safe. I'd never been in this room before, and at first all I could do was stare in awe at the fish swimming just out of our reach.

Wella shut the door, leaving me with Carth. He gave me one of his flirty grins and offered his hand. "Alone at last."

I slid my hand into his much larger one, entwining our fingers together as we stepped forward along the raised path to the bed. Now that I knew something of what to expect during my bonding, it was hard not to rush forward.

"I've wanted to do this for a long time," Carth said, as we reached the bed. I'd changed from my traveling clothes into a long, silken dress in dark blue, and he took his time letting his gaze move down my curves. "You're gorgeous. I could look upon you for hours. Days. Years. And never grow tired."

"You're such a charmer." I stepped closer to him. "But is there anything real behind that flirtatious smile?"

He pressed a hand to his chest. "You wound me. I have never told you a lie."

"No, but I'm not the only one you flirt with, and I know you've shared a bed with many ladies before me."

"Only to practice for this moment." He slid his arms

around my waist. "From now on the one bed I'll be sharing is yours."

Our lips met and his tongue danced inside mine, while his fingers slid across my breasts, making my nipples instantly hard. With a groan, he tugged the dress up and over my head, revealing my naked skin. I wore nothing underneath in anticipation of this moment, and was rewarded with a guttural sound in his throat as he looked at me.

"Get in the pool," he said, while he began removing his own shirt. "We'll save the bed for later."

While watching him undress, I walked over and put my toes in the pool beside the bed. It was just deep enough for me to sit down in, and as soon as Carth had his pants unlaced, I dropped down into it.

"It's so much warmer than I expected," I said as I sank into the pool.

Carth sat on the platform beside me and put his feet in the water. He was fully naked now, and I admired the body that so many women had coveted before me. Sculpted muscle, but different from Erroh's somehow. While Erroh had a soldier's body, Carth was leaner, his body developed from years of swimming, with the tan skin and sandy hair to match. The large cock jutting up between his legs was also quite impressive.

The water suddenly leaped up and washed over my shoulders, while Carth gave me a wry grin. His eyes roamed over my body, and wherever he looked, water rushed over me. It spent a lot of time on my breasts, and I couldn't help but moan as the water tickled, then squeezed, then ran in circles around my nipples. Even without touching me, Carth knew how to drive me wild.

I reached over and wrapped my fingers around Carth's hard cock, the long rod giving a different feel in my hands than Erroh's had. The soreness from my first time had passed, leaving excitement in its place. Our mouths met again, our kiss passionate and demanding, while I stroked his length.

Water rushed between my legs, caressing and teasing, but it wasn't enough. "Carth, please," I said with desperation.

He dove into the water toward me, pulling me into his arms while his mouth fell on my neck. Pressure between my legs made me part them, and as soon as I did, the water rushed around our naked bodies, pressing us closer together. I wrapped my legs around his hips, while his fingers cupped my bottom.

He guided his cock to my entrance, then rubbed it against my folds to make me moan in desire. As my fingers dug into his skin, he sank inside me slowly, with a sigh of great satisfaction.

"Gods, you are so snug," he said, as he filled me to the hilt. He felt different than Erroh, though I wasn't sure how exactly, but I loved the contrast anyway. A girl would never get bored with four lovers, that was for sure. Or five, for that matter.

The water pushed us together, holding me up and

giving him leverage to move in and out of me. Waves rippled around us as our bodies rocked together. I threw my head back and held on to him while he pumped into my core. His mouth found my neck and discovered a spot below my ear that had me moaning hard.

Then his speed increased, to my intense delight. Every thrust made my body respond with passion and pleasure. The water surged around me, stroking my ass, between my thighs, around my nipples, hitting me everywhere, allowing Carth to touch me in ways I'd never imagined.

My release built slowly, with pleasure rushing through my body like a stream, and then a river, and then a waterfall.

"Carth, more," I moaned when the feeling of release eluded me.

He moved faster, then took one hand off of my hip to tease the little nub that evoked such strong orgasms, as Erroh and I had discovered. At the same time, water rubbed my tight hole in the back, in an area no man had touched before. I cried out, grasping at his shoulders to try to center myself as I came apart.

He pulled me close and thrust deep as he came inside me. As we both surged together, the water around us shot straight up in the air, and then ice began to form along our skin. It completely covered us, locking us together, while waves of pleasure spread through us. All we could do was kiss and ride it out.

After the water receded and the ice melted away, I wrapped my arms around Carth and breathed in his scent, committing our first time to memory—one I'd never forget. Making love in the water was certainly an exhilarating experience, especially when he used his magic at the same time.

"How did you learn how to do all that with the water?" I asked.

"I've been practicing—alone, mind you—ever since I got these powers" He gave me a sensual grin. "If they can't be used for sex, then why bother having them at all?"

I laughed, as he picked me up and grabbed a nearby towel, wrapping me up in it. Then he set me down on the bed and crawled up beside me, folding his arms under his head.

"The Water God should appear to us now, probably in the ocean there." I rested my head on his shoulder and gazed at the school of fish swimming by.

"Somehow I don't think he's coming."

"Me neither."

Carth wrapped an arm tightly around me. "That's all right. I'm sure I can keep you entertained." Then he paused. "Although I should have asked this earlier. Do we need to worry about pregnancy?"

"No. One of the benefits of being the Ascendant is there is no chance of a surprise pregnancy. I will have one daughter in ten years, like my mother did, and that girl will replace me when the time comes."

"Which means you can have as much sex as you want until then," he said, pulling me on top of his growing cock.

I laughed. "And you're obviously eager to provide it."

"It's my job to please the woman I love, is it not?"

"I suppose it is." I bent my head to kiss him.

The Water God never arrived, but we managed to find plenty of ways to keep ourselves occupied, until we finally fell asleep.

CHAPTER TWELVE

The journey back to Soulspire was faster and easier now that Carth was a dragon too. Erroh spent a few hours showing Carth the basics before we left the Water Temple, and then they took turns flying us until we reached the palace.

When we landed in the castle garden, Varek was waiting for us, along with Parin and Zain. My other mates did not look pleased that he was there, and I shared their sentiment.

Carth set down on the ground and let out a roar, spreading his blue wings wide, and Zain gave him an approving nod. I quickly hugged Zain and Parin, and then turned to my fifth mate. "What brings you to the palace you hate so much?"

Varek snorted. "Sorry to disturb you, princess, but I have news about the Unseen."

"It's the only reason we let him inside," Parin said, eyeing Varek with disdain.

I tried not to bristle at Varek's nickname. "Continue."

"As suspected, the rally you witnessed near my bar was a recruitment effort on their part. They've been holding them all over the city, and rumor is they're spreading outside Soulspire too."

"Do so many people hate the elementals and the Dragons?" Erroh asked.

Varek shrugged. "They make some good points about the inequality among humans and elementals, but I'm not going to stand back and let them attack us again. I know I run in some questionable circles, and many may think—" He shot my other mates a wry look. "That I'm only a criminal, but I have a line I won't cross. I'm pretty sure they do not."

I crossed my arms, feeling exhausted after our long journey. "Do you have any actual information?"

Varek clenched his jaw. "I was getting to that. I sent some of my people to join their cult to gather information. They say the Unseen have something planned, something big they want to show everyone."

"What do you suspect?" Parin asked.

"I believe the Unseen are somehow stealing elemental powers, but I'm not sure how."

"That should be impossible," I said, but then remembered what my mother had said. "Although you might be correct. We've had reports of missing elementals."

"If they are stealing elemental powers, we need to stop them immediately," Zain said.

"There's an Unseen meeting at midnight tonight at the old warehouse that burned down at the northern end of Soulspire," Varek said. "We can sneak in and learn more then."

"I know the place," Erroh said. "But can we trust a criminal?"

Carth crossed his arms. "I'm with Erroh, I'm not sure we should work with a man with his...connections."

"My connections saved you once already," Varek snapped. "While you've been off having sex in fancy temples, I've been investigating these cultists. You wouldn't know anything about them if not for me."

"Or maybe this is some kind of trap," Zain said.

"Believe what you want." Varek spread his hands. "I'll be at the meeting. You can join me if you wish, or I can handle things on my own. Your choice."

"We'll be there," I said, the words slipping out of my mouth immediately. My mates didn't trust the man, and in many ways I didn't either, but I believed he was helping us. I felt it in my gut.

Of course, I'd seen him do some seriously heinous things in my dreams. He couldn't explain away cold-blooded murder. I wouldn't forget that either.

Parin cleared his throat. "We appreciate any accurate information you can give us."

"Come inside," I told my five mates. "We can speak more privately in our chambers."

"As you wish, princess," Varek said, but his inflection had changed. The offensive pet name didn't have the same level of vinegar in it this time.

We headed inside the palace and got many looks from the guards as Varek walked with us to the other wing. Then we entered our communal dining room and sat down to a huge meal. I wanted to kiss the cooks for having food ready even though they didn't know when we'd return. My parents were still gone, and the responsibility of dealing with the Unseen was firmly on our shoulders. I'd be able to form a plan for infiltrating the meeting a lot better with a full stomach, and hopefully my mates would be less grumpy about Varek's presence too.

At least he was here in the palace. That was a start.

Varek didn't stay long. During our meal we sketched out a rough strategy, and then he headed back into the city with plans to meet us at the warehouse after dark. He said he would procure us some masks too.

We were relying on him a lot for this mission. I hoped it wasn't a mistake.

I borrowed a dress from a servant and donned my black cloak, before heading out. I was far too recognizable in Soulspire, but hopefully with a mask and my hair under a hood, I could avoid notice. My other mates were similarly dressed in plain clothes, including Carth, who had to borrow something from Erroh.

We split up into two groups to travel in different paths to the location. A woman with four men might be a little too obvious. Of course, my mates tried to talk me out of going, until we were standing outside the building that had once housed a large warehouse before a fire destroyed it years ago. A fire that was caused by elementals. The irony was not lost upon me.

As we moved down an alley toward the back entrance, a large man suddenly stepped out of the shadows directly in front of us. I jumped, along with Erroh and Parin at my back, all of us reaching for our weapons, but then I recognized Varek.

"Are you trying to get yourself stabbed?" Erroh asked.

"Put these on." Varek held out three gray masks toward us. "The password to enter is 'nameless.' We'll go in two at a time, or our number will draw suspicion."

"The others?" I asked. Zain and Carth had taken the shorter route to the warehouse.

"Already inside. The meeting is starting soon."

I donned the mask with a nod, then pulled the hood up to cover my hair. Parin stayed back with Varek, while Erroh and I approached the metal door and knocked.

A slat opened at the top of it. Eyes peered out. Waiting. Watching.

"Nameless," Erroh said.

The slat shut, and then the door opened. We stepped into a dark hallway with stale air, the walls blackened and charred in places. A large man grunted and gestured for us to move forward.

The hallway opened up to a big room filled with people, most of them wearing gray masks, though some didn't bother. A large wooden stage had been set up on one end, and more masked people waited there, along with something big and boxy that was covered by a black cloth. A large crate maybe?

I gazed around the room, sizing up the audience. So many people, a lot more than I expected, all crowded together and eager for this meeting to start. My mates were among them somewhere, but I couldn't pick them out with the masks on. At least I had Erroh at my side.

The masked people on stage suddenly clapped their hands three times, making the room go quiet as everyone realized the meeting was starting. One of them stepped forward, wearing a black mask.

"We are the Unseen, but we will not be ignored any longer," the person said in a booming voice, repeating a phrase I'd heard at the rally. The voice sounded vaguely feminine, but I recognized she was trying hard to deepen and alter her tone. Probably for anonymity. "We applaud your bravery for meeting us here tonight, for recognizing the inequality humans face every single day, and for being willing to put an end to it through whatever means necessary. It's time to put humans first again."

My stomach twisted as people in the crowd raised their fists and chanted, "Humans first, humans first, humans first!"

The leader raised her hands and flames burst forth from them, causing the audience to settle down again. "For years, we've been powerless against the elementals and the Dragons, but no longer. We've discovered a way to gain magic ourselves, and tonight we will demonstrate for you. Soon, we will be equal to the elementals...and then the Dragons themselves!"

The crowd surged forward in anticipation and I was shuffled along too, anxious to see whatever they were about to do to gain magic. As I watched, the leader nodded at some of the other masked figures, who yanked off the cloth. Underneath it was four cages, and inside them were elementals—one of each type. They were in bad shape too, the fire elemental's flames dim, the water elemental's body too thin, the earth elemental's rock body partly smashed, and the air elemental little more than a wisp. I couldn't help but gasp in horror at the sight, and quickly covered my mouth. Something terrible was about to happen. I needed to stop it, but I had to know what they were doing too.

"Do we have a volunteer?" the leader asked.

Dozens of people raised their hands, and she chose a young woman with red hair who wasn't wearing a mask, then asked her, "What type of magic would you like? Earth, air, fire, or water?"

The redhead glanced between the elementals with excitement in her eyes. "I think... air. Yes, air."

"A fine choice." The leader stepped toward the cage with the air elemental, who floated backward as she approached, but there was nowhere to go. "Step forward, initiate."

The redhead moved closer, and the leader took her hand, before reaching toward the elemental with her other one. Dark tendrils lashed out from her fingertips and sank into the air elemental's chest, causing it to scream, a sound like a whirling tornado. It struggled and fought, but the iron cage kept it contained and unable to use its magic.

"No!" I yelled, rushing forward.

A strong hand clamped down on my arm, holding me back. I glanced over my shoulder and saw black hair. Varek.

"Don't do anything stupid," he hissed.

"I have to stop this!" It was my duty to protect those elementals from the humans, and vice versa. I couldn't stand back and do nothing as they hurt it.

As I struggled to get closer, the leader's dark tendrils yanked out something from inside the elemental, a swirling vortex of glowing yellow air, and shoved it into the redhead's chest. The air elemental immediately dissipated, vanishing before our eyes as it passed away. A yellow glow surrounded the redhead for a brief second, before fading.

"You now have the powers of an air elemental," the leader said. "Try them."

The redhead looked uncertain, but she waved her hand

and a breeze went through the room. The crowd erupted into a loud cheer, stomping and hollering, and the woman cracked a huge smile.

The leader gave her a nod. "You are one of us now. We will train you in how to use your new magic to defend humankind and take back the world."

"Thank you," the woman said, and another masked member led her away.

The leader gazed back at the crowd. "I need another volunteer."

This time just about everyone's hand raised. It made me sick. Did no one care that this was murder?

I wasn't going to stand around and let this happen. It was time to end this meeting and free these elementals. I shrugged Varek's hand off my arm and used my air magic to lift me up toward the ceiling, then used my newest elemental magic to spray water down on everyone, drenching the crowd. People screamed and looked up.

I yanked off my mask as I hovered over them. "What you're doing is murder and I won't let this continue! Free the elementals now!"

"It's the Dragon spawn!" the leader yelled. "They're here to stop us from gaining the power that should be ours, but we will not be stopped!"

She launched fire at me, and I stopped it with a blast of water magic. Erroh flew up next to me, while my other mates surged through the crowd toward the remaining cages. They knew what to do—freeing the elementals was our number one priority.

Most of the crowd screamed and fled in a panic, but many of the people on stage started fighting us back with their elemental magic. There was not enough space for Erroh or Carth to become dragons with so many people running around, so Erroh and I fought from the air, while my other three mates climbed the stage. Zain and Varek used fire and death magic to stop some of the cultists, while Carth ran to the first cage and freed the elementals.

It was total chaos in the warehouse. I didn't want to hurt anyone in the crowd who wasn't attacking us, but it was hard to know who had magic and who didn't. I tried to go after the leader, but she'd vanished into the crowd at some point.

Soon the warehouse was empty except for the five of us, a few cultists we'd knocked out, and the freed elementals, who I immediately began healing as best I could. The Silver Guard showed up, hearing the commotion, but by then it was over. The leader and most of the cultists had fled, but at least the other three elementals were safe.

And now we knew why they were going missing.

CHAPTER THIRTEEN

The elementals were escorted back to the palace by the Silver Guard, where our staff began taking care of them immediately. The few cultists we captured were dragged off for interrogation, but I doubted they'd give us much information. Varek left to try and track down the Unseen's leader, while the rest of us returned to our quarters in the palace.

As we entered our communal area, I slumped down on the sofa, feeling defeated. Yes, we'd rescued three of the elementals, but we'd failed to save the fourth, and everything I'd seen and heard tonight had left me shaken.

"I need to contact my parents and tell them we know why the elementals are going missing," I said.

"I can't believe the Unseen would go to these lengths," Parin said, shaking his head. "It's barbaric."

Zain sat on the sofa beside me, moving stiffly. "People will do many things to gain power. Especially when they feel they have none."

"Are you all right?" I asked, noting the way he held his side.

"I'm fine."

"Let me see," I demanded. "If you're injured, I can heal you."

He moved his hand, and it came away bloody, but he shrugged. "One of the Unseen had a large knife."

Carth rolled his eyes. "That's why you use your magic to keep them away."

"I was trying not to burn the entire place down a second time," Zain said. "Fire is different from air or water or even earth. You need precise control. You can't just throw it around and hope for the best."

"He does have a point," Erroh said.

"Nice to see you've learned something in your training sessions," Parin muttered.

I rose to my feet. "Let's go into my quarters. The rest of you, get me some cloths and a bowl of water."

Zain stood and winced, and I took his hand and practically dragged him onto the bed, after setting down a towel underneath him.

"Off with your shirt," I ordered.

Zain leaned back on my pillows. "You're bossy when someone is injured."

When he unlaced his shirt too slowly, I grew impatient and reached over to help. Even though I was worried about him, I couldn't help but enjoy the sight as I bared his chest. He was exquisite, his body toned from being a guard at the Fire Temple.

As soon as I saw the cut on his side, my focus went entirely to it. He winced as I prodded it, but didn't make a peep. "It's long and deep. I bet it hurts a lot."

"I've had more enjoyable nights, it's true," Zain said in a clenched tone.

"Why didn't you say anything sooner?"

"It was more important for you to heal the elementals."

Pressing my hand to the wound, I sent healing life energy into it. While I did, Parin and Erroh returned with some cloths, while Carth brought me a bowl of water. I sent them away after that so I could concentrate.

Under my care, the injury slowly disappeared. When I was finished, I grabbed the cloth and carefully cleaned the blood off of Zain. "Here," I held out my hand. "Sit up, let's get this shirt off to be cleaned. It's covered in your blood."

"I can do it now." Zain sat up without difficulty and shrugged the torn shirt off his shoulders. "But the shirt is ruined."

"I can't heal it as easily as I did you," I told him with a smile.

"Thank you." Zain leaned forward and took the cloth from me, throwing it into the basin. He put his hands on my shoulders. His lips neared mine, and I couldn't slow the race of my heart.

My healing must've been effective because he pulled me close and rolled us, so I was suddenly on my back on the bed, with him looming over me. His mouth came down on mine hard and his tongue tangled with mine. When he pulled back, I was breathless and hot with desire. The evidence of his arousal was pressed into my core too. He pushed it harder against me, and I moaned and arched up against him.

"We can't do this until we get to the temple," I whispered.

He flexed his hips and his hard length rubbed against me, pressing into my little nub that was so eager for his attention. My moan turned breathy and I spread my legs, giving him more access to grind against me, even as I said, "This can't go any further. We don't know if the Gods would be angered."

"The Gods have deserted us, have they not?" he replied, then to my shock and delight, sank his teeth into my neck just enough to harden my nipples pressed against his chest.

I was seconds from giving in when the door was flung open. Carth bounded into the room. "Break it up, you two. No naughty business until we get to the Fire Temple."

The others followed him inside, and Zain and I reluctantly broke apart. My mates all draped themselves on my bed like they belonged there, except Parin, who stood apart with his arms crossed. He still didn't feel like one of us.

"We need to talk about your actions earlier," he said.

"What do you mean?" I asked, sitting up and trying to ignore the wetness between my legs.

"You were pretty reckless at the meeting," Erroh said.

"I had to stop them from killing another elemental!" I glanced between them. "Do you not agree?"

"Of course we do," Carth said. "They had to be stopped. But we were split up from you and couldn't protect you."

Zain took my chin in his hand. "If you ever do something like that again without a second thought to your own well-being again, I'll..."

I arched one eyebrow. "You'll what?"

"Yeah, what will you do?" Carth asked with a grin. "Turn her over your knee and give her a spanking?"

Erroh doubled over laughing. "No, she might enjoy that too much."

I rolled my eyes, even as heat flared between my thighs. Welcome to life with four mates. "I appreciate your desire to protect me, but don't forget I've spent my entire life training for this role under the current Dragons. I can handle myself in combat."

Parin cleared his throat and shifted like he was uncomfortable. "We need to figure out a plan for dealing with the Unseen."

"Varek is trying to get more information for us," I said. "He proved to be trustworthy tonight, so we have to believe he will continue helping us. I will send a message to my mother about the kidnapped elementals too."

"We should continue to the Fire Temple," Zain said, and gave me a heated look. "It's more important than ever for us to be at our full strength now."

I nodded, and swallowed my desire before it overwhelmed me. "We'll leave tomorrow."

CHAPTER FOURTEEN

I n the morning, we set off for the Fire Temple.

Parin stayed behind to see what he could learn about the Unseen, to oversee the protection of the kidnapped elementals, and to fill in my parents if they returned before we did.

Carth and Erroh both stayed in dragon form for the entire trip, except for when we stopped to eat or take a break. The journey took most of the day, although the Fire Temple was the shortest distance from Soulspire, at least when flying. Zain and I alternated riding the two dragons, giving the other one time to practice flying maneuvers. We could have had a dragon each to ride, but out of an unspoken agreement we decided to sit together. I liked having his arms around me and his hard chest against my back. I also liked when his hands spread down to cup my breasts or idly stroke my thighs.

As the sun set, the land underneath us changed to a desolate expanse of earth turned black by previously spilled lava. The volcano, Valefire, loomed before us with smoke rising from its mound, and I glimpsed the ocean behind it. We flew over vents in the ground shooting up steam and boiling water, and as we approached, the air grew thick with heat and humidity, along with the smell of rotten eggs.

Zain's hands tightened around my waist. "It's good to be home."

We landed on the top of the volcano, which was flat and smooth before dropping off into a huge crater in the center. A glowing light came from within it, and Mom told me that was where the Fire God had appeared to them. I wondered if he would make an appearance for us, or if Zain was right and the Gods had abandoned us. Hearing him, my most devout mate, say such a thing had been disturbing...but I feared he might be right.

The Fire Temple stood before us and was made of glossy black obsidian and featured huge pointed towers. Two women emerged from the tall door at the front, both wearing black silk robes with red trim. One was Zain's mother, High Priestess Oria, and the other was his grandmother Calla, who had been High Priestess during my mother's Ascension. Orla had the same nearly-white hair as Zain, and Calla's hair had once been blond but had turned white with age. She held onto Oria's arm for support as they moved toward us.

"Mother, grandmother," Zain said. "I'm pleased to announce I am Sora's fire mate."

"We've heard." Oria held out her arms, and Zain hugged her. "We're so proud. I prayed you would be chosen, and I'm pleased the Fire God listened."

"I prayed as well," Zain said.

"Zain," Calla said with a giant smile as she embraced him. "I'm happy to see you on this joyous day."

"And you, grandmother. None of this would have been possible without you."

"Our family has always served the Fire God, and it pleases me that you will continue that tradition." She patted his cheek and then turned to me.

I bowed my head in respect. "High Priestesses."

Calla took my hand. "I'm so pleased things happened this way. You've always been the granddaughter of my heart, but now it's official."

My heart warmed at her words. She'd been like a grand-mother to me as well, even though we were not related. When I was very small, if my parents needed to leave me to go on some diplomatic mission or another, they'd always left me with Calla, first in the Fire Temple, and then in Spark-port after she retired as High Priestess.

"We've prepared the bonding room for you," Oria said, as she led us inside to a large entry with a statue of a dragon. "Would you like to share a meal first?"

"No, thank you," I said, glancing at Zain. He nodded. Neither one of us wanted to wait any longer.

"We've already eaten, but we'd enjoy sharing a meal with you in the morning," Zain said diplomatically.

In the entryway, we briefly said hello to Zain's four fathers who all told him how proud they were, before they took Erroh and Carth to their own rooms.

We didn't have to go anywhere—the bonding room was just on the other side of a tall door in here, which was carved with two dragons. Oria and Calla both gave us knowing smiles and bowed their heads, as we stepped inside.

The bonding room had a domed ceiling, flickering torches, and the large bed I'd come to expect. But I barely had time to look around before Zain reached for me.

There were no nerves. No hesitation. No need to speak. I didn't care about the dust we'd picked up or how wild my hair was. As soon as the door closed behind us, we launched ourselves at one another, removing our clothes as quickly as we could.

"Later I will take the time to savor you slowly," Zain said, between passionate, hungry kisses. "Being the third of your mates has been torture. I can't wait any longer."

"I can't wait either. I've wanted to do this since we kissed a year ago."

His hand slid down to my breast, recreating the moment when we'd shared a forbidden kiss in the dark halls of the temple, only to never speak of it again. Until now—when we were finally allowed to be together.

We fell on the bed together, in the same position we'd been interrupted in the night before. Desire raced through me, this time hotter, brighter. I spread my legs and grabbed his hard cock. His girth was impressive, more than either Carth or Erroh, though not quite as long. As I guided him to my entrance, eager to feel him move inside me, I couldn't help but wonder what it would be like to be with all three men at once.

But when he pushed into me, all thoughts vanished. Throwing myself back on the bed, I moaned at the feel of him filling me, stretching me.

Zain moved fast, pulling me into his arms and thrusting into me over and over. I clenched around him when he slipped a hand between us to press against me, knowing exactly where to go and what to do.

Then he rolled us over on the silk sheets, putting me on top. After sleeping with two other men a few times, I knew what to do now, and I rolled my hips while he pinched my nipples. It felt good to take control and chase my own pleasure, especially when I could see how much it excited him too.

In the hot, humid room, sweat poured out of me, slicking my body against his so that each slide was an erotic massage. His hands clenched my behind and guided me faster, harder, urging me on while I threw my head back and let go.

My cry of pleasure echoed through the obsidian chamber as the orgasm burned through me. My inner walls clenched of their own volition, milking Zain and bringing his climax too. As we both came together, fire burst out of his skin and soon engulfed me, spreading through me like I was a dry forest full of kindling. I knew now this was how our bond was formed, and how I gained his powers, but it was still shocking to have flames rippling across my naked skin.

Then the fire died out, and we clung to each other while we caught our breath. The heat inside me slowly quieted until the sweat dried on my skin.

"I love you," Zain murmured against my ear, as he stroked my back.

"I love you too."

He sat up and reached for his clothes. "Come. Let's see if we can lure the Fire God from the volcano."

There was a door on the other side of the room that Zain opened, and it took us back outside, this time near the crater in the volcano. The heat grew more intense here, but the volcano was not erupting right now, so we had little to fear as we approached.

Zain stood before the glowing crater and raised his arms. "Fire God, we have come for your blessing. Please honor your devoted servants with your presence."

He was laying it on thick, but waiting around for the Gods in the other temples hadn't worked. Maybe this would. Mother had told me the Gods had just showed up, but things had changed since then. My Ascension was proving to be very different from hers.

"We beseech you," Zain called out. "Show yourself!"

Nothing happened.

I let out a long sigh. "He isn't coming. As you said, the Gods have abandoned us."

"I thought, out of all your mates, I would be the one who could summon a God." A heavy frown settled on his face. "I've failed, like the others."

"I'm sorry." I took his hand. "It isn't your fault. None of us know why they're not appearing, but the Fire God chose you for a reason. He knew you were my perfect mate. Focus on that."

He slowly nodded. "I can do that."

We went back inside the bonding room, and he focused on me for the rest of the night. It was enough to almost make my worries about the Gods vanish completely...but not quite.

CHAPTER FIFTEEN

In the morning we had a nice breakfast with Zain's family, and then we stepped outside so he could shift into a dragon for the first time. Everyone applauded and cheered as blood red scales covered his body and grew into wings, and then he launched into the air. He had a moment where he took a dive and nearly fell, but Erroh and Carth were there to lift him up with some wind magic and give him a few pointers.

We returned to the palace that evening, and Parin rushed out to meet us when we returned. His face showed obvious distress, and I quickly slid off Zain's back and asked, "What is it? Is something wrong?"

"I'm glad you're back so soon," he said. "We have a problem."

As my other mates returned to their human form, they gathered close. "Tell us," Zain demanded.

"A large delegation of elementals was supposed to arrive this morning from Divine Isle. They've been visiting each Realm, trying to continue to foster good relations between the humans and the elementals, as your mother requested."

"Let me guess," Carth said. "They never arrived."

"Indeed. No one has heard anything from them in days."

"Perhaps they're simply delayed," Erroh said, though he didn't sound like he believed that.

"Have any of my parents returned yet?" I asked, as my stomach became leaden with dread. We all knew what had happened to the elementals, even if we hoped that wasn't the case.

"Unfortunately, no," Parin said.

My mouth twisted into a grimace. "We'll have to handle this on our own then. Is there anything else you can tell us? How many there were? Where were they coming from?"

"They were coming from the Air Realm. I believe there were about twenty-five of them."

"That's twenty-five more people who could have magic soon," Zain said.

I turned toward my three bonded mates. "Do the three of you feel up to flying again?"

Erroh puffed out his chest. "I could fly all night long without a problem."

Carth rolled his eyes. "We'll be fine. We can investigate the elementals' journey, retrace their steps as best we can, and see if we find anything."

"Thank you," I said. "Are you sure you'll be all right?"

All three men swore they were fine and would leave immediately after grabbing some dinner from the kitchen. Flying made you very hungry.

My heart sank a bit as they walked away. I didn't like the idea of being away from them, but it was necessary to find anything we could about that missing delegation.

I turned toward Parin. "I'm going to visit Varek and see if he's learned anything new."

Parin's brow furrowed. "Would you like me to come with you?"

"No, although I appreciate you asking, instead of demanding you're going to protect me."

"You're a formidable woman, Sora. I've come to realize that over the last few days."

His words gave me a bit of hope. Maybe he no longer saw me as just a little sister anymore?

"Besides," he continued. "Although I don't approve of Varek's lifestyle, he has proved useful. We need whatever information we can get from him."

"I agree." I tentatively reached out and took his hand. "Thank you for taking care of things while we were gone."

Parin glanced down at our linked fingers, and then gave my hand a squeeze. "I'm happy to help however I can."

I leaned close and pressed a light kiss to his check. "Please stay here in case the elementals or my parents arrive. I'll be back as soon as I can."

I didn't waste any time rushing out to find Varek. An entire envoy of missing elementals was enough to make my blood run cold. If the Unseen took all their powers, we would be vastly outnumbered in a fight. The delegation had to be found immediately.

Remembering Varek's words about being discreet, I went to the back door of the Lone Wolf Pub, the one he'd led me out of last time. Once there, I knocked sharply, keeping my head down and my hood pulled low over my face. I couldn't risk getting caught alone by the Unseen.

Varek's sister, whose name I vaguely remembered was Wrill, opened the door with a sneer. I was starting to think that was her permanent expression. "The princess was returned."

"I need to speak with Varek."

She stepped aside to let me in. "We knew you'd come crawling back for more."

"He is my mate," I snapped. What was her problem with me? "I didn't choose him, but I have to make the best of it. As does he."

She tossed her black hair. "Go on then. You know where to find him."

Ignoring all the other doors, I headed straight for Varek's office. I considered going right in, but took a deep breath and knocked instead. Just because Wrill was rude and condescending didn't mean I needed to be too.

"Enter," he barked.

I stepped inside, and saw him standing beside his desk. He was shirtless and slightly sweaty, rubbing a cloth along the back of his neck, and I was momentarily stunned by the sight of all those muscles and tattoos. I had the strongest desire to run my hands down his chest and trace every dark line of ink.

When he saw it was me, a slow grin spread across his face. "A visit from the princess. Is it time for our bonding?"

"No, although I'm sure you wish it was." My gaze snapped back to his face as I tried to focus on why I was here. "A delegation of elementals went missing, and we suspect the Unseen have taken them. Have you heard anything about that?"

"I have not."

I sighed and tried again. "Have you learned anything new about the Unseen since we last spoke?"

"No, but my people are still working on it." He tilted his head and studied me. "That's not the real reason you came here though, and we both know it."

The way he said it sent heat to my core, but I refused to let him affect me that way. "It's time you moved to the castle and became one of my mates in more than just name. We need your help with the Unseen, and that will be easier if you're beside us."

He stalked across the room, until he was standing right in front of me, and I couldn't help but look at his naked chest again. "Or maybe you just want me near you."

"It wouldn't hurt for us to get to know each other better," I admitted.

"We know everything we need." His hand reached up and slid behind my neck, and I thought he would pull me in for a kiss, but he only gazed into my eyes. "I'll make you a deal. Fight me in the ring. I want to see if you're as good as the stories say. If you win, I'll move to the palace and be the good little mate you want."

That sounded too good to be true, considering it was unlikely he'd win. "And if I lose?"

"You get on your knees and suck my cock until my seed spurts down your throat. Then you call me your king."

My eyes widened at his vulgar words and shocking demands. His fingers tightened in my hair and his dark eyes roamed down my body, making it clear he planned to win. I tried not to show the way my body responded to his rough, demanding touch, and to the thought of wrapping my lips around his cock. I shouldn't have wanted him so badly, but I couldn't help myself.

"Deal," I said, my voice breathless.

A wicked grin crossed his lips as he let go of me. "Follow me, princess."

He led us to the door I'd peered inside the first time I came to his bar. The door opened into the massive room, where two men were fighting while a small crowd watched.

"Everyone out," Varek's voice boomed. No one argued or even hesitated. They grabbed their things and headed out the door, only pausing to give him nods of respect.

When the last person had exited and we were alone, we both stepped into the ring painted on the floor. Torchlight flickered across Varek's chest as he faced me. I loosened my shoulders and rolled my head, ready to fight. I couldn't lose this one.

"No weapons, no magic," he said. "We fight until one of us concedes defeat or is forced out of the ring."

"Agreed."

Varek went immediately on the offensive. He ran straight for me but was easy to dodge. We spent a few minutes going back and forth that way, each of us easily ducking and darting away from the other.

I spread my arms, taunting him. "We can't do this all day."

"Indeed." Without warning, he changed his tactic, rushing toward me with impressive speed and force. I barely managed to avoid his blow, but I was able to use his momentum to spin around and kick him in the face. He stumbled back, then wiped a tiny spot of blood of his lip with a grin.

Then it got interesting. He'd been toying with me before, but now he truly came after me. I had to admit, his abilities were a real test of my skills. I'd previously thought only the best of the Silver Guard was a match for me, including Erroh. Now I had to add Varek to that short list too.

As we moved around the ring, exchanging blows and occasionally grappling with our bodies pressed close together, I began to wonder if I was going to lose. Would I have to return to my mates knowing I'd sucked the cock of the city's number one criminal?

That couldn't happen, no matter how excited the thought made me. I redoubled my efforts, flinging Varek to the ground and landing on top of him as I tried to get a grip on his arms.

But he threw me off, and the next thing I knew, it was me on the bottom. His bigger size pinned me down, and his hard body pressed against mine. A slow smile crept across his face, and his lips came down to my ear. "I think you like this a little too much."

With a grunt, I swung my leg around and wrapped it around his neck, twirling both of us until I was on top again. Straddling his waist, I fought the desire that rushed through me as I held him down. "Submit."

"Never." He gripped my hips, rubbing his cock against me once, and then shoved me off him.

We both scrambled back to our feet, breathing heavily, and not just from the exertion. When we faced each other this time, it was with hunger in our eyes too. My gaze fell to the large bulge in his pants.

Maybe losing wouldn't be so bad after all.

He used my distraction against me and managed to grab my waist, lift me up, and nearly throw me out of the ring. I got away just in time, then launched a series of sharp kicks and blows against him. When he came at me again, I back up right to the edge and used a move Jasin had taught me, dropping down and sweeping my leg under Varek. He toppled over, knocking me down with him, but only he was over the line. We both saw it at the same time, and a huge grin spread across my face.

I stood and offered him my hand. "I win."

He stared at my hand for a second, before taking it and letting me help him to his feet. Then he yanked me toward him and captured my mouth in a rough kiss. His other hand gripped my behind and pulled me hard against him, while my heart raced. My fingers gripped his muscular upper arms, squeezing them, while he ravished my mouth. I wondered if he would do the same to my body when the time came.

"I let you win." He took my chin in his hand. "But one day you're still going to suck my cock and call me your king."

I stared back at him defiantly, even as my body arched toward his touch. "Not likely."

"We both know you want it as much as I do." He released me and called out, "Wrill!"

She stepped into the room and glowered at me. "Yes, brother?"

He wiped sweat off his brow and stalked toward the door. "I'm moving into the palace tonight."

"You...what?" She blinked at him.

"The princess needs my services." He rested a hand on her shoulder. "Though it pains me to leave the Quickblades, I'm placing you in charge of them."

"Brother, this is madness. You built this organization. You can't leave it now for some...woman."

"The Death Goddess chose me, and I have to accept my role as Sora's mate. I'll make sure no one questions your command, and I have faith that you will lead the Quickblades well."

She stammered, but then nodded with a grim set to her features. "I'll do my best."

Varek turned back to me. "I need to take care of a few things here tonight, but I'll have my things brought to the palace in the morning. Does that suit you, princess?"

"That's fine." I was shocked he was actually fulfilling his part of the deal, and going beyond it at that. I'd asked him to move into the palace, but hadn't said anything about giving up the Quickblades. Maybe he was finally starting to realize he had a higher purpose as one of my Dragons.

CHAPTER SIXTEEN

V arek moved all his things into the palace the next morning. Ever since we discovered I had a fifth mate the staff had been busy getting a room ready for him, even adding a new door so it connected to our main living space. They weren't sure how to decorate it—how did one represent the Death Goddess, with skulls and black curtains?— but I'd told them to leave it fairly plain so Varek could put his own touches on it.

Parin watched Varek move in with a tight-lipped expression, his arms crossed. I wasn't sure if any of my mates would ever be able to accept Varek, even after he gave up his criminal lifestyle. I wasn't sure I could accept him either. My body responded to him, but if we were going to be bound together for the rest of our lives, I needed more than that.

Varek didn't even have time to unpack his belongings

before Carth and Zain returned. We had a balcony outside our communal area that was large enough for two dragons to land on at once, and we met them out there under the midday sun.

I rushed toward them and lovingly touched both their dragon snouts, relieved to see them unharmed. "Did you find anything? Where's Erroh?"

"We found the site of the ambush in the Air Realm," Zain said. "The elementals were smart and left scorch marks along the ground, leading to what we think is the Unseen's current hideout. It's an old barn on a farm that's long abandoned. Erroh stayed behind to watch them in case they move again."

"How far away?" Parin asked.

"Too far to walk," Carth said. "Are your parents back?"

I shook my head. "Unfortunately not."

"We'll have to do this on our own," Varek said.

Both dragons swung their heads toward him, their fangs flashing. "What are you doing here?" Zain asked.

Varek gave him an icy look. "I live here now."

"Varek's given up his position in the Quickblades and has moved into the palace," I said.

"About time you conceded defeat," Carth said, then snorted.

"I did no such thing," Varek snapped.

I pressed my palm to my forehead. "Enough. Carth and Zain, you should grab some food quickly to recover your strength, while the rest of us prepare to leave. We'll go as soon as we can to rescue those elementals."

We arrived at the location about an hour later, with me and Parin riding Zain, and Varek riding Carth. No one was pleased about the seating arrangements, but we had bigger things to worry about.

Since showing up as dragons would be a little too obvious, we stopped a short distance away and my mates reverted to their human forms. From there, we crept through the woods until we found the tree Erroh was hiding in, which had a good view of the barn. He did a doubletake when he saw Varek with us.

"Has anything changed?" Carth asked.

"No," Erroh said. "No one has gone in or out."

"Are we certain the elementals are inside?" Parin asked.

"No, but it's the only lead we have," Zain said.

I surveyed the barn. It was obviously abandoned and much of it had already collapsed, except for a large section on one side that appeared intact. That's where the Unseen had to be holding the elementals. "An ambush seems like the best option. Quick and fast."

"I have another idea," Varek said. "I can summon a group of shades and send them in to distract the people inside, and possibly cause them to run out in fear."

"You can summon shades?" I asked, horrified. Shades

were minions of the Death Goddess who hungered for life. Like elementals, they could only be harmed by earth, air, fire, and water—weapons did nothing to them. They could also turn both invisible and intangible, making them especially deadly to humans. My parents had made it one of their missions to make sure there were none left in the four Realms. "Why didn't you mention that before?"

"I can do many things." Varek leveled an intense stare at me. "I knew this one would offend your delicate sensibilities."

"I don't like it," Parin said. "Shades are...unnatural."

"And creepy," Erroh added.

"Do you have an alternative plan?" Varek asked.

"We could shift into dragons, fly in, and tear the place apart," Carth said.

I debated it, but then shook my head. "Too dangerous. The elementals might get hurt. Better if the cultists don't know we're here at first."

Varek raised his chin. "Then we go with my plan."

I sighed. Sending in shades to do this felt wrong, but we needed whatever advantage we could get in this fight. "Yes, fine, summon your shades."

Varek stepped into the woods a short distance away from us and spread his arms, his eyes closed. As we watched, ten shades rose up out of the earth, floating into existence in front of us. They appeared to be made of shadow and were only vaguely human-like, with glowing yellow eyes and sharp claws.

A shiver ran down my spine. Varek may have been one of my mates, but that didn't make the shades any less unsettling. I wondered what Mom would think of me agreeing to such a horrible thing. Would she consider it worth it to save these elementals and prevent more humans from stealing magic?

Varek whispered something to the shades, and they headed for the barn. From our hiding spot behind some trees and bushes, we watched the shades float to the side of the barn and then glide through it, as if the walls weren't even there.

The screams started only moments later. Gods, what had we done?

We used the distraction to surround the barn's entrance. The door flew open and people began to run outside to escape the shades. As they did, Parin used an earthquake to knock them off their feet, while Erroh had the same effect with a huge blast of air. When Carth saw someone throwing fire, he blasted them with water. The next person that came out of the barn sent jets of water toward us, which Zain quickly extinguished.

I used the distraction to step inside the barn, which looked a lot better on the inside than the outside—it was clear they'd cleaned up in here when they'd made it one of their hideouts. The shades were attacking the cultists, but the humans were fighting back with magic. Everywhere I looked I saw flashes of fire and water, and many of the shades were already vanquished. Even worse, I spotted a dozen cages set up around the room, like the one at the demonstration the other night. They were all empty.

We were too late.

I didn't have time to mourn, because a piece of the fallen roof launched itself toward me, no doubt thrown by one of the cultists. I used air magic to redirect it, then turned to face the person who'd attacked me. The woman in the black mask. Before I could react, she launched a fireball at me, along with a shard of ice. I quickly used fire and water to stop the attack without hesitation, but then gaped at the cultist standing before me. Had she really used both fire *and* water?

"How?" I asked.

A harsh feminine laugh came from behind the black mask as she threw a blast of air at me. "Yes, I do have all four elements...and more."

After I dodged the air blast, a bolt of darkness snaked out from her hand toward me. It looked like the same shadowy mass that the shades were made out of, the same thing she'd used to steal magic from the elementals. I blasted it with fire, though I was still new to using the element, and my control was weak. I ended up spraying wide, setting the floor on fire beside her. The flames quickly jumped high, and I lost her in them.

Carth appeared beside me and quickly put out the flames with a spray of water. There was no sign of the woman in the black mask. We ran outside, where most of the fighting had moved. I expected my mates to be in dragon form taking people down, but none of them were. Most of the cultists had either fled, or were dead or captured. The shades were gone.

"Fly above and search for the leader!" I told them. "She can't have gotten far."

"We can't," Erroh said, as he held a few cultists in a hurricane-like whirlwind.

"Can't?" I asked.

"None of us can shift," Zain said.

I glanced between all of them to confirm. "How?"

No one had an answer. My mates continued to subdue the remaining cultists that fought us, and I stared as Varek reached out with that same shadowy power to grab three people in front of him and suck the life from their bodies.

I gazed out at the forest, cursing myself for letting the leader get away. She was damn good with her magic and she had more elemental powers than I did, since she also had earth. But she had something else too. Something I didn't have—but Varek did.

When the fighting ended, we began to investigate the barn and the area around it. Now that it was empty I spotted a lot more things I hadn't noticed before, like four strange pillars at each outside corner of the barn, covered in inky black ooze, with the four elemental symbols carved on the side and a skull on top.

"This is what is stopping our shifting," Erroh said with a shudder. "It feels horrible just being near it."

"The Death Goddess is involved somehow," I said.

"That's her magic on these pillars, and I'm pretty sure the leader has it too."

All eyes turned to Varek, who shrugged. "I don't know anything more than you do."

"Is this some kind of trick?" Erroh asked.

"Yeah, are you double-crossing us?" Carth added.

Varek huffed. "I've done nothing but help you and fight by your side, and you still don't trust me. Enough. Figure this one out on your own."

He turned on his heel and stomped away, into the forest. I had no idea if he'd head back to the palace, or if we'd just lost any ground I'd previously gained with him.

I sighed. "The Death Goddess is obviously helping the cultists, but that doesn't mean Varek is too."

"We know that, but we need to be careful too." Parin gestured at the pillars. "Especially with things like this in play."

"Let's destroy it," Zain said.

He unleashed magic at the pillar, but it seemed to absorb it. Magic wouldn't work against it. Just like it prevented anyone nearby from shifting into dragon form.

"I'll send the Silver Guard to see what they can do," Erroh said. "For now, let's get out of here."

We moved back into the forest, until my mates claimed to not feel the effects of the pillars anymore. Then I sagged against the nearest tree. "The elementals are all dead. The Unseen's leader has all four elements. We failed."

Erroh leaned beside me. "We did the best we could, and we'll be better prepared next time."

"If it weren't for those pillars, we would have stopped them," Carth said.

I knew they were trying to make me feel better, but they were wrong. We'd never stood a chance today—and now we'd lost Varek too.

CHAPTER SEVENTEEN

When we returned to the palace, Varek was nowhere to be found. His things were still there, his bags half unpacked, but there was no sign of him.

We'd gathered up the few prisoners at the barn, but there were more dead than captured. The rest had fled. The cultists the Silver Guard imprisoned would be questioned, but we already knew from previous attempts that they wouldn't talk. They were too devoted to their cause.

My parents returned that afternoon from Divine Isle, and I was forced to explain everything that had happened while they were gone. Getting the words out was difficult. I felt like the biggest failure ever. How was I supposed to take over for my Mom when I couldn't even protect a few elementals?

When I'd finished, Mom surprised me with a tight hug.

"You've done the best you could in a difficult situation," she said. "I'm proud of you."

"There's nothing to be proud of," I said, bowing my head.

"Of course there is," Slade said, resting a hand on my back. "You handled everything that happened just as we would have done."

I wasn't sure I believed that, but it didn't matter, because they were back now. It was such a relief to know they'd returned and could help with this problem. And to think only weeks ago I'd been eager to be the Ascendant, and believed I was more than ready to take on any challenge. Now I realized how foolish I'd been.

I wasn't ready. Not even close.

We were in my parents' living room, where I'd spent many days and nights with them before. Mom sat beside me on a sofa, with Slade standing beside us. Reven leaned against the nearest wall, while Auric sat in a nearby chair and Jasin paced restlessly.

"I'll have my spies try to uncover more information about the Unseen," Reven said.

Auric rubbed his chin. "We can't let those cultists murder any more elementals. Tensions are already high with the elementals at the moment."

"I'll set up extra guards around the city," Jasin said.

Kira nodded. "I'll speak with the elemental ambassadors and advise them to be especially cautious due to a radical human group."

"Is there anything I can do?" I asked. "Or my mates?"

Mom offered me a warm smile. "Thank you for the offer, but I think it's best if you continue your training and focus on growing closer with your mates. How are things going with them?"

"Things are good with Erroh, Carth, and Zain. I bonded with them at their temples and feel confident about them as my mates." I hesitated. "The other two...are more complicated."

"That's why it's especially important to spend some time with them now." She kissed my cheek. "Go and be with them. We'll take care of everything else."

"Thank you, Mom."

When I returned to my quarters, it was time for supper, but I found my three dragons passed out in exhaustion. They'd been doing a lot of flying and fighting, so I guess I couldn't blame them. I hoped to spend some time with Parin instead, but a member of the staff informed me he'd gone to visit his sister and her baby. I took supper alone in my room and went over some of the books we had about the Death Goddess, looking for any information that might help us.

A knock on my door made me jump, and I realized I'd fallen asleep with my face in a book. I quickly tamped down my unruly curls and went to open the door. "Yes?"

To my surprise, Varek stood on the other side. His long black hair was wet, as was his clothing, due to the soft rain outside. "May I come in?"

His unexpected politeness left me speechless, but I

nodded and stood back. He swept into my room, his large masculine presence filling it completely.

"I wasn't sure if you were going to return," I said softly, surprised at how relieved I felt to have him here again.

"We made a deal, and despite what you think, I am a man of my word."

"I'm pleased to hear it."

He gave me a short nod. "I've been out searching for answers. I know your mates—and you, probably—don't trust me, but I have nothing to do with the Unseen."

I stepped closer to him, unable to stop myself. "I believe you. Do you know how their leader is using death magic?"

"I have my suspicions, but I'm not ready to share them yet. Not until I'm sure."

I bit my lip and considered pressing the issue, but then decided not to push him. We were already in an awkward place with each other, and I didn't want to make things worse. I needed him to become part of the team.

"All right," I said. "In the morning, we're going to begin training together. If we can't fight as a group, we're not going to be able to defeat the Unseen, and that includes you too. We can't always rely on the shades to give us an edge."

He arched a dark eyebrow. "I'm fine with that, but are your other mates?"

"They don't get a choice in the matter."

A wry grin split across his lush lips. "I like a woman who's not afraid to boss her men around. Just as long as you realize that won't work on me."

"Won't it?" I asked, with a challenge in my eyes.

"A king doesn't take commands, he gives them." He took my chin and kissed me hard, plundering my mouth with his tongue, until I was gasping with desire. Then he stepped back and headed to the door. "I'll see you tomorrow for training."

And just like that, he'd left me speechless again.

Training with all five of my mates began the next morning. As we stood out in the field, under a sky taunting us with the chance of rain, I sensed my bonded mates' apprehension. Now that we were mated, I could feel some emotions from Erroh, Carth, and Zain. It would only grow stronger in time, but for now it was more of a tingle and a clear sense they weren't all that happy about Varek being among us. I couldn't feel emotions from Varek or Parin yet, but their crossed arms, scowls, and stiff body language said they weren't best pleased either.

"I'm not sure how exactly you'd like me to train with the others," Varek said, gesturing at my mates. "If I use my magic on them, they'll die. That's the nature of it."

"Is there anything you can do that isn't, well...deadly?" I asked.

"No. Is there anything you can do with life magic that isn't healing?"

I sighed, but he had a fair point. "Fine, then you'll focus

on combat training and deflecting the others' magic. Later, we can run the Gauntlet too."

We split up into pairs, with plans to rotate throughout the day. I was especially keen to work on my fire magic, but Zain was still a beginner too. If we weren't careful, we'd burn the palace down. I'd have to ask my fathers to join us tomorrow.

Instead, I practiced air against Parin and water against Zain. I'd grown up watching my dads using their powers, and even though I hadn't had any magic of my own yet, I'd studied every movement they made. Maybe it was because of that subconscious training that I picked up magic easily once I actually gained it. I felt like I'd been using it my entire life, and had only now unlocked my full potential.

Or almost full, anyway. I wouldn't be a dragon until I bonded with my other mates and gained their powers too.

Parin was next. I watched him spar with Varek, using his weapon of choice, a staff. He had been trained in combat, like we all had, but he was a diplomat, not a real fighter. Varek took him down easily, but as I watched, he reached out and shook Parin's hand after the match. Maybe there was some hope for them yet.

Erroh stood beside me as we watched them start another match. "I notice you haven't been pushing to go to the Earth Temple," he said.

"No, I thought we could all use some time together first." I turned toward him. "Plus, I needed to get used to the idea of Parin as my mate. Are you still upset he was chosen?"

"A little." Erroh rubbed the back of his neck. "Is it strange that my brother will share your bed, as I do? Yes. But I've started to accept it. I can tell he cares about you, in his own rigid way. It could be much worse."

I couldn't help but laugh. "High praise there."

He took my hand. "I want whatever makes you happy. If that's my brother, then that's fine. If that's Varek... well, I'll accept that too."

I pressed a kiss to his lips. "Thank you."

He grinned and stepped back, then created a tornado between us. "Now, back to work. See if you can dissolve this."

We continued practicing every day for a week against each other, trying to hone our skills so we could go up against the Unseen again. Next time we would be better prepared. My fathers came out to the field and gave us tips too, and by the end of the week, I could use fire without being a hazard to myself and others.

During meals, Erroh, Carth, and Zain joked around like the friends they were. Varek and Parin were still separate from them, not joining in on the fun, except one time I caught them rolling their eyes in unison when the other three were being particularly ridiculous. Progress.

In the evenings, one of my bonded mates came to my bed. It was nice not sleeping alone anymore, and I began to wonder what it would be like to have multiple men in my bed too. Would that ever happen?

On the last night of the week, Parin cleared his throat and said, "Now that we are confident about working together and your parents are here to continue the investigations into the Unseen, I think it's an appropriate time to make our way to the Earth Temple."

Carth nudged Zain with a huge grin. "I told you he'd bring it up first."

Zain grumbled and pulled out a coin, slamming it on the table. "Fine."

"You were betting on this?" I asked, my eyebrows jumping up.

"Just a bit of fun." Carth shoved the coin in his pocket, his eyes dancing. "I bet he'd crack by the end of the week, unable to resist Sora any longer. Zain thought Sora would demand to go first."

Parin looked away at that, as did Erroh. I wasn't sure how to respond either. Yes, I wanted to bond with Parin. I'd always been attracted to him. Plus I wanted to gain my powers and unlock Parin's true potential as a dragon. But I'd been waiting because I wasn't sure how he felt about me and didn't want to rush things.

Varek leaned forward with a grin and broke the awkward silence. "You made a bet and didn't include me? For shame."

The tension broke and Zain said, "Next time."

"None of you should be making bets," I said, rolling my eyes. "But yes, I do agree it's time to go to the Earth Temple. The Unseen could attack again at any moment, and it's best if we're better prepared for them."

I'd put off the next journey as long as I could. We'd hurt The Unseen with our attack, but as much as Reven's spies searched, not another whisper was heard about the cultists. If Varek knew anything, he was keeping silent.

But bonding with Parin meant bonding with Varek next. I wasn't sure I'd ever be ready for that.

CHAPTER EIGHTEEN

The journey to the Earth Temple was the longest of them all. It was a good thing my mates had been practicing flying. My parents offered to take us to the temple, but we declined, saying it would be better for us to do this on our own, and they were needed to defend the elementals against the Unseen.

This time, everyone came with me and Parin, except Varek, who said he still had business in the city. The dragons traded off flying to conserve their strength, and Parin held me stiffly the entire time. I tried to relax and enjoy being in his arms, but it didn't work. I was too nervous he was only doing this because he had no other choice.

As we flew, Parin pointed out places of interest. As a diplomat to the Earth Realm, he knew much about its history, even things my parents had never told me. At least our flight wasn't boring.

It took us three days to reach Frostmount, the tallest mountain in the Earth Realm, located far in the north. The air was freezing, especially up this high, but we'd all donned warmer clothes this morning in preparation. We glided over the snow-covered mountains until we saw Frostmount ahead of us, with the Earth Temple at the top.

Unlike the other temples, this one was not a building but more of a cave inside the mountain. It had been destroyed by my grandparents, led by The Black Dragon, much like they'd destroyed the Air Temple. Slade and the new High Priestess, Parin's aunt Stina, recreated the temple with their earth magic many years ago. However, they couldn't make up for the battle that had happened here—the one that cost Parin's father his life.

High Priestess Stina met us just inside the cave entrance. She had the same rich, dark skin that Parin had, along with thick dark hair touched by gray and big brown eyes. She threw her arms around Parin and laughed.

"How lucky to have my own grandson chosen by the Earth God! Ah, and Sora, always good to see you. And you too, Erroh, I swear you look bigger than when I last saw you." Stina gave another hug to Parin, then went to Erroh and patted his cheek. Her brother had been Parin's father, which meant she wasn't related to Erroh, though they had a good relationship. "I know you're probably eager for the bonding, but I made your favorite meal."

"I could never turn your beef stew down, Aunt Stina," Parin said.

"Good. You can tell me all about how the Gods chose two brothers for Sora's mates. I've never heard of such a thing before!"

The two brothers shared a look, before trudging forward. It was obvious they both had zero desire to discuss this topic. At least they were united on that front.

The Earth Temple had always been my favorite, and I tuned out their conversation to gaze around the great cave. The walls were unnaturally smooth due to earth magic, and embedded inside them were hundreds of glittering crystals. The flickering candlelight made them look like shimmering jewels, casting a rainbow of colors along the stone floor and the large jade green dragon statue we passed.

Stina spent the entire dinner digging for information, while her priests looked on with enjoyment. It was abundantly clear she was amused by the unconventional relationship that included both half-brothers. I humored her and explained that none of us really had much of a choice. The Gods chose for us, and she couldn't argue with that.

When supper was over, Stina and her priests stood, and she spread her arms. "And now we shall take you to the bonding chamber."

Erroh cleared his throat and looked away. "I think I'll head to bed early. Good luck, and all that."

Parin nodded to him with a pinched expression, and then we turned away and headed down a tunnel to the bonding chamber. Inside there were even more crystals, casting rainbows around the room like shadow. Otherwise the large room was pretty plain, with only a bed and some stone tables beside it.

"This room is beautiful." I ran my hands along the wall. Warm energy caressed my skin as I felt the power within the crystals. "I've always loved the Earth Temple."

"Me too." Parin sat on the edge of the bed, his movements stiff. He looked like he would rather be anywhere else. "Sometimes I like to imagine my father here, and what it was like for him to grow up within these walls."

Well, that made me feel like a total fool. I should've been more aware of how being here might affect Parin. His father died here, after all. A father he'd never even met.

Before I knew it, I'd crossed the room to put my hand on his arm. He studied it for several moments, then took my hand and pulled me down to sit beside him on the bed.

"How often did you visit here as a child?" I asked.

"About once a year. My mom always came to pay her respects and mourn my father, even after she married Erroh's dad. She also wanted me to have a good relationship with my aunt. Mostly for Stina. I'm the only thing left of her brother, after all."

"Does it bother you to be here?" I asked.

"Not at all." He tilted his head up and studied the crystals. "At first, I was shocked when the Earth God chose me. I didn't want such a position, not when it would take me away from my duties as a diplomat. Now I've decided it's the perfect way to honor my father and his sacrifice, while continuing to foster diplomacy in the four Realms."

"I'm sure he would be proud of you."

"I hope so."

When he looked at me with warmth in his eyes, I decided to try something. Scooting closer, I put my hand on his knee and leaned forward, pressing my lips to his. He stiffened before wrapping his arms around me, but his kiss was light and hesitant.

I pulled back, my cheeks burning up. "I'm sorry. I shouldn't have done that."

"No, don't apologize. It's what we came for after all."

"Yes, but..." I sucked in a sharp breath. "I know you don't see me that way, and that's okay. We just have to get through this once, and we don't have to do it again."

Parin's face softened. "That's not what I want. Yes, I used to see you as something like a little sister, but more than that, I always saw you as completely off-limits. You were Erroh's more than mine. It's taken me some time to adjust my thinking."

"I understand."

"Are you all right with this? I never asked before, but I am ten years older than you, after all. Does it bother you?"

"No." I ducked my head, unable to look at him. "I've always had something of a crush on you, even though I never dreamed being with you would be possible, for so many reasons. When you were chosen I was shocked, but excited too."

"Truly? I was never sure if you saw me that way."

I laughed. "I also wasn't sure how you felt about me."

"What a pair we are. Both of us wondering if the other wanted this or not."

"To be fair, our lives have been chaotic since we found out. We've barely had time to sit down and really talk."

"Then let's talk." He brushed the back of my knuckles with his thumb. "We don't have to do the bonding tonight. We can spend time getting to know one another. As equals."

"I'd like that."

We talked for hours, long into the night. He asked me questions about my wants and dreams. We discussed our favorite foods, colors, and hobbies. I learned he'd previously been with a woman for three years in a serious relationship, but she disliked how often he had to travel for work. She left him two years ago for a man in the Silver Guard, and he'd been alone since. In fact, he'd sworn off relationships, having decided they weren't for him, until the Earth God told him he had a different fate.

When I yawned, he looked at the pillows. "I will be a perfect gentleman if you'd like to settle in. I can sleep on the floor."

"I'm sorry. I didn't realize how tired I was. It's probably best if we get some sleep."

He averted his eyes as I took off my traveling clothes and put on the silky gown I'd brought to sleep in. When I was settled under the soft brown blankets, I sat up and looked at him. He'd removed his clothes and stood in his linen shorts and my mouth fell open. I'd never seen Parin shitless before, and the reflected light from the crystals made his dark skin gleam, highlighting his frame. He wasn't as muscular as my other mates, but he was large and toned...and beautiful.

He was about to spread a blanket on the floor when I said his name. "Parin," I said softly. "Come sleep here."

He looked back and forth for a moment, then dipped his head. "Thank you."

I pulled the blankets up to my chin and tried not to obviously stare at him as he slid under them beside me. The heat of his body spread under the covers, chasing away the heavy chill in the air. I used air magic to blow out many of the candles in the room, covering us in darkness, and then we both said goodnight.

I kept waiting for his breathing to shallow and even out, but it never did. He shifted from his back to his side, facing me, and caught me looking at him in the dim light. Too late for me to pretend to be asleep.

Scooting under the covers, I shifted closer to him. Parin lifted the blankets so I could move my head to his pillow. My body wasn't pressed against his, but brushed against him in several spots, sending shivers of anticipation through me.

Something had changed during our conversation. I began to see him as something different. Not Erroh's brother. Not the older boy who always tried to keep me out of trouble. Not a forbidden crush.

A man. An attractive, virile man.

The tension had evaporated between us, and I pressed my lips to his again. This time they softened around mine, caressing and pressing, stealing my breath.

His large hand slid up my bare arm to my neck, changing the angle of the kiss. Parin's tongue slipped through the seam of my lips and I parted them, eager to see what he wanted to do with that tongue.

His tongue turned out to be my favorite feature of his. He kissed his way down my cheek, his hand still on my neck. Then he settled me back against the pillows as his lips and tongue made their way to my shoulders. He used his free hand to slide the flimsy strap of the nightgown down my shoulder. I pulled my arm out, but froze as his hand traced the collar of the gown. He pulled the other strap down, then tugged the material below my breasts.

I gasped when my nipples hit the cold air. Parin grunted and moved lower, his tongue circling one nipple, while his warm palm covered the other. He continued this amazing torment, slowly covering my breasts with his tongue, before moving to my belly, and then lower, lower, lower. Between my legs. Parting them wide.

His head moved between my thighs, and he showed me just how amazing his tongue truly was. Licking, sucking, teasing, until I was crying out his name and gripping the pillows hard.

"Parin, please," I cried. "I need you inside me."

He moved up my body and settled between my legs. The head of his cock pressed against me, inducing shivers of anticipation from me. His eyes met mine in the dim light, and he kissed me tenderly as his cock breached my entrance.

He sank into me slowly. I watched his face as he pushed in. He looked...content.

"Sora," he gasped.

"I feel it too," I whispered. The connection with him came quickly, and was deep and steady, like the earth. It wouldn't be shaken by any small force. Parin was my rock.

I allowed myself to close my eyes and focus on the connection with him as he moved in and out of me. Slowly at first, then faster and harder. He ground into me, until an orgasm spread deep through me, making my body tighten around him. His hips rocked into me as he came too, and the ground around us rumbled and shook. Under my fingertips his skin turned to stone, including the hard cock inside me, but then the magic spread across my skin too. It held us there like a statue of a couple caught in the act of lovemaking, before fading away.

We both relaxed on the bed, sated and satisfied, and I rolled over and snuggled close. Parin looked at me in surprise, and then his expression turned pleased. We both knew the Earth God wasn't coming, so there was no sense getting dressed or waiting for him. He wrapped his arms around me and pulled me onto his chest.

I slept like a rock.

CHAPTER NINETEEN

In the morning we decided not to rush back to the city, and instead to take some time to practice our magic and give Parin space to learn to fly. As the Earth Dragon, flying would be most difficult for him, at least according to my father, Slade. Their deep connection to the ground made it harder for them to embrace the sky.

After a hearty breakfast, we headed outside into the freezing air, trudging through the snow on the mountain, and then began to practice our magic. I reached for the earth and made it shake, then loosened some stones and raised them in the air. I now had all four of the main elements in my control. This was when I should have been able to ask the Life Goddess for her blessing, except I'd been given a fifth mate. My own dragon form would have to wait a little longer, unfortunately.

Erroh clapped Parin on the back. "Come on, big brother. For once I can teach you a thing or two."

Parin grunted and then shifted into his dragon form. He was the largest of all my dragons, with a stout body and dark hunter green scales that looked almost black, until the sun hit them.

Zain, Carth, and Erroh shifted too, my four dragons all spreading their wings before me. I couldn't help but smile, even as I felt a pang of jealousy. More than that though, I felt a strong love and deep affection for them. I could sense through the bond how happy they were and how close they felt to each other too. Even Parin—he was truly one of them now.

With the help of my other mates, Parin managed to lift off the ground, though it wasn't easy at first. His aunt and her priests whooped and cheered as his wings stretched above us and he flew circles around the Earth Temple.

Now I only had one more mate to bond with...but he would be a challenge.

As we approached Soulspire a few days later, the smoke was the first sign that something was wrong. "Hurry!" I yelled to Erroh, whose back I rode. As the Air Dragon he was the fastest, even while carrying me, and he zoomed ahead of the others. Zain and Carth were just behind us, with Parin at the rear.

161

Thick plumes of smoke shot up from various parts of the city. We flew toward the nearest one, and saw it was a hotel specializing in hosting elementals, now on fire. The Unseen had attacked again. Except this time there were dead humans in the street too, including some of the Silver Guard. Carth let out a roar and sprayed water on the flames, dousing the building, but it was too late. The battle here was already over.

We flew across the city, over other places the Unseen had attacked, and a pattern emerged—every place had been one that catered to elementals. I spotted my fathers helping out at the various spots, and it was a relief to see they were safe. There was no sign of my mother, however. My dads would never be out there if she was injured though, so she was probably busy dealing with the aftermath of the attack elsewhere.

When we came to a spot near Varek's bar, we spotted him outside a café that had crumbled down like an earthquake had demolished it. He was speaking to one of the Silver Guard and pointing, but he turned toward us as we landed.

"What happened?" I asked.

Varek's face was grim, and I noticed exhaustion in his eyes. "The Unseen attacked locations around the city where the elementals were known to gather. There were so many of the cultists, the elementals and the Silver Guard didn't stand a chance. Your parents and I came out here to help, but by then it was too late. Many elementals and guards were already dead. Some elementals were kidnapped."

"How could they have done this?" Zain asked.

"I thought we'd weakened them a lot," Erroh added.

Varek shook his head and looked away. "Their numbers have grown considerably."

"Where is my mother?" I asked.

"She's set up an infirmary in the palace and is healing people there."

I nodded, since it was exactly what I'd expect. "I should go do that too. The rest of you, please see how you can help my fathers throughout the city."

"Wait," Varek said, raising a hand to stop us.

"What is it?" Parin asked.

Varek's jaw clenched. "Nothing. We can speak on it later."

"You know something, don't you?" Carth asked.

I took a step toward Varek. "You've kept a secret too long. It's time you told us."

"I think I know who the Unseen's leader is and how she has Death Magic." He drew in a sharp breath. "It's my twin sister, Wrill."

"You're twins?" I asked.

He nodded. "Born only minutes apart. I believe when the Death Goddess gave me her power, she bestowed it upon my twin too."

"She can't have two champions!" Zain said.

Varek shrugged. "I don't think the Death Goddess cares

about playing by the rules. If it's true, then Wrill has all the same powers I do, but with no duty to become Sora's mate."

"Why didn't you tell us sooner?" Parin asked. "We could have prevented all this."

"I didn't believe it at first. I also knew if I told you before I was sure, you'd rush in and do something rash. I wanted to be certain."

"And you're certain now?" Erroh asked.

"Fairly. I've been trying to find Wrill for the last few days so I could talk to her, but she's gone into hiding."

"And you put her in charge of the Quickblades," I said, as the true horror of Wrill as the Unseen's leader settled in.

Varek's frown deepened. "Unfortunately, yes. Hence the bolstered numbers today. She's using them for her cause."

I sighed. "We'll discuss this later. For now we need to deal with the aftermath of these attacks and get the city back in order."

My mates agreed with me, and we split up to do our duty. My heart was heavy as I returned to the palace and found the infirmary. Tears sprang to my eyes when I saw the number of injured humans and elementals in the room. This was my fault. I should have made Varek tell me his suspicions instead of giving him space. I should have dealt with the cultists before going to the Earth Temple. I should have done a better job of being the protector of the four Realms.

I hadn't been the Ascendant for very long, and already I'd failed miserably.

~

I healed alongside my mother all through the afternoon and into the night. At some point I passed out in a chair in the corner, planning to only take a five minute nap, and I woke when someone picked me up. My eyes cracked open and I was startled to find myself in Varek's strong arms, cradled against his hard chest. He didn't look at me as he carried me through the palace, and he ignored my sleepy protests that I was fine and could continue healing.

Finally he set me down in my bed. "You need to rest."

I tried to hide a yawn. "You can't tell me what to do."

He spread his arms wide. "By all means, get up and walk out this door. I won't stop you."

I couldn't do it. Exhaustion had turned my limbs to heavy weights, and the thought of moving them seemed impossible.

I didn't know if I responded or not. I'd like to think I replied with some clever quip, but it was more likely I fell asleep immediately. Next thing I knew, it was morning, and one of the servants was quietly bringing me some food and water. I devoured both, needing sustenance after using so much energy to heal people. I wanted to get back to the patients immediately, although by the time I'd fallen asleep, everyone who was injured had already been attended to by myself or my mom.

After a quick bath, I received a summons from my parents, and met them in their living room again. All five of them looked weary. It was strange to see, as I'd always viewed them as unstoppable and indestructible. Now I was beginning to understand the pressure they'd been under my entire life.

Mom looked especially tired and was eating fruit from a tray when I entered. She patted the spot on the couch beside her. "I'm sorry to summon you like this, Sora, but it's important."

I sat beside her and stole some of the fruit from her tray. "What is it?"

"I think you should go to the Death Temple with all haste and complete your bonding."

If my mouth hadn't been full of melon, my jaw would've dropped. I hadn't expected her to encourage me to mate with Varek.

I swallowed. "Are you sure?"

"I do. Your fathers and I are not happy about the Death Goddess involving herself, but you've decided to accept him as your mate, and there's nothing we can do at this point unless we wish to start a war against the Realm of the Dead."

I settled back against her pillows. "No, we don't want that. We have enough problems at the moment."

"I saw Varek carry you to your room last night," Jasin said. "I appreciate that he seems to care for you, but you must be cautious. There was a reason I never could find proof about his criminal enterprises, and it's not that he was innocent."

"I know. I am. But he's given up all of that." I hesitated,

but then decided not to tell them about Wrill. Not until we had more information. "He's helping us uncover the source of the Unseen's powers and we should know more soon."

"It's very disturbing that the Death Goddess is helping them," Auric said, rubbing his chin. "Especially since the other Gods have abandoned us."

"There must be an explanation for their absence," Slade said.

Mom stared out the window in thought. "Perhaps they've taken a step back from the world, entrusting us to handle things ourselves."

"They should at least give us their blessing." My head dropped. "I would have liked to meet them."

Mom wrapped her arm around me and gave me a squeeze. "I'm sorry. Perhaps they will come to you once all of the bonding is complete and the Life Goddess gives you her blessing. Even more reason for you to go to the Death Temple immediately."

Reven crossed his arms and spoke from his spot against the wall. "If she isn't ready, we shouldn't push her. Let Sora choose her own path."

I gave him a grateful smile. "Thanks, Dad. I think I'm ready, but I don't want to leave the city yet. There could be more attacks at any moment, and it's my duty to protect the people."

"We will be here to defend the city," Jasin said. "Don't worry about that."

Auric reached over and patted my hand. "You'll be able

to help the people even more once you have your dragon form."

"I'm with Reven, there is no reason to rush this," Slade said. "Sora, go whenever you are ready. If it's tomorrow, fine. If it's a year from now, so be it."

"We only want whatever is best for you, of course," Kira said. "And we believe in you."

"I want to do my part to help the people," I said. "I'll speak with Varek and see if we're ready. If not, we will continue our training and help defend the city."

All of my parents seem satisfied with that answer, and I went to the infirmary to check on the patients still there. Most of them had recovered, and the rest I did some more healing on. When I was finished, I returned to my rooms and collapsed.

A tingle down my spine woke me sometime later, when night had fallen. The room was pitch black, except for a tiny sliver of moonlight, and silent except for the lightest footfall. I sat up quickly, just in time to dodge a blade made of ice. Above me, I saw a smooth black mask.

The leader of the Unseen had come to kill me.

CHAPTER TWENTY

The door burst open and Varek swooped inside, wielding a large knife. He immediately leaped forward and put himself between me and the attacker, then grabbed her by the arms.

"What are you doing?" he demanded, his voice angry.

Flames danced across the Unseen leader's skin and Varek was forced to let her go. I blasted her with water to douse the flames, then used air to circle her like a hurricane. When Varek got to his feet, he reached through the torrent of water and air and grabbed her mask, yanking it from her face.

I let my magic go with a gasp when I saw Varek's twin standing before him. We'd suspected it was her, but seeing the truth was still shocking. Especially since she'd just tried to assassinate me in my sleep.

"I knew it." Varek threw the mask aside in disgust. "I just hoped I was wrong."

Wrill looked up at her brother with an angry slant to her mouth, but made no move to attack again. "You shouldn't have stopped me."

"What were you thinking?" he asked. I'd never seen his face so raw, utterly stripped of all the walls and masks he put up to keep himself aloof. "Sneaking in here to try to kill my mate? How could you?"

Wrill's gaze moved from him to me, and murder glinted in her eyes. "I did it for you, brother. If she's dead, you don't have to mate with her and become the thing we hate the most—a Dragon. How could I? How could *you?*"

"The Death Goddess chose me. She set me on this path. I could not refuse." His eyes flicked to me. "Nor do I want to."

She lurched forward and took his hands in her own. "Varek, please. There's still time to change your fate. Walk away from this. Return to the Quickblades. Help me run the Unseen." Her eyes gleamed with hope and righteousness. "We're doing great work. Righting the balance between humans and elementals. You can be a part of that too."

He shook his head. "What you're doing is wrong. Yes, there is a power imbalance, but murdering elementals is not the way."

"We're changing things," she snapped. "You can either be a part of that change, or you can be the enemy."

"I am where I am meant to be."

Wrill glared at him and then turned it to me. "Then you've chosen to side with the oppressors. So be it."

She leaped out the open window into the night, and then used air to lift her up and fly away. Varek and I rushed after her, but then we stopped. Varek didn't want to go after his own sister, and even if I could catch her, what would I do? Kill my mate's sister? Lock her up?

All I knew was that this new development wasn't going to make our bonding any easier.

My bedroom door burst open and my other mates rushed in wielding weapons. They looked around, but saw only me and Varek standing there, and then relaxed.

"We heard a commotion," Zain asked. "Is everything all right?"

"Yes, we're fine," I said, though I was still a bit shaken by everything that had happened.

Varek's jaw clenched. "The leader of the Unseen is my sister. We've confirmed it now."

"She was here?" Erroh asked.

"She tried to kill Sora."

"She did what?" Carth asked, and the other men echoed his statement.

I held up a hand. "It didn't work, obviously. We stopped her and no one was injured. At least now we know for sure it is her."

"We need to double your guards," Parin said. "No one should have been able to get in here."

"My sister has control of all four elements, plus death

magic," Varek said. "She is almost unstoppable. More guards won't help much."

He was right. Wrill was the dark version of me, with death magic instead of life. My equal, at least until I bonded with Varek, gained his death magic, and then became a dragon myself. Only then could I have any hope of defeating her one-on-one.

"I'd like to speak with Varek alone, please," I told my mates.

Erroh nodded. "We'll patrol the area in case other members of the Unseen are about."

My other mates headed out the door with him. As soon as it was shut, I let out a long sigh, feeling exhausted again. I sat on the edge of the bed and looked up at Varek, who stared out the window where his sister had vanished.

"I can't believe she came here to kill you." He shook his head. "I knew she was the leader of the Unseen and what she was doing, but I never thought she would go so far."

"Why does she hate the Dragons so much?" I was especially curious since she'd implied Varek hated them too.

"Our childhood did not leave us with much love for the Dragons. Or the elementals."

"Tell me."

"Very well, but it's not a nice tale." He pulled out a chair from my desk and sat in it, facing me. "Our father was a general in the Onyx Army. He was killed in the last battle against the Black Dragon."

That meant he was one of the men that fought against my parents—and lost. "I'm sorry. I had no idea."

"Wrill and I were only two at the time. When the new regime took over, my mother was left a widow with two small children. No one would help her, because of who her husband was and how he'd died. The Onyx Army was disbanded and disgraced. She tried to find work, and often took in sewing and laundry, but it wasn't enough. She even applied here at the palace, but was turned away."

My heart broke, imagining a tiny Varek coming to the palace with his mother, looking for help. "That's awful."

"She was young and pretty though, so she had one other way to make money. A way I preferred to pretend weren't happening." He scowled as he stared off into space. "She got involved with some bad people and got hooked on alcohol. Wrill and I were on our own for the most part, growing up on the streets, and I did everything I could to take care of my mother and my sister."

"That must have been difficult for all of you," I said.

He shrugged. "There are many who went through similar things when your parents took over. It wasn't an easy transition for anyone who supported the Black Dragon."

I bowed my head. "I...I had no idea."

"Of course not. You grew up in a palace with everyone telling you how special you are." His voice was harsh, but then he paused and sucked in a breath. "As I was saying, things were tough for us, but we managed. Our mom took a new job with some elementals, helping them as an assistant in the warehouse. Then one of them lost their temper and burned the place down. She died from the smoke."

I gasped and covered my mouth. "That's horrible. Was it the same warehouse where the Unseen had their meeting?"

"Yes. That's when I began to suspect it was Wrill. We were thirteen when Mom died, and she never got over it. She blamed the Dragons for our father's death, and the elementals for our mother's."

"That does explain a lot." I sighed. "Do you blame us also?"

He gazed at me for an eternity. "No," he finally said. "Perhaps I did once. But not anymore. Otherwise I wouldn't be here now."

I let out a relieved breath. "Good."

"After my mother passed, I did whatever I could to take care of Wrill. Many of the things I did were...not exactly legal. Before I knew it, I had people working for me. I formed the Quickblades, with Wrill at my side. Though you think we're nothing more than criminals, we did have a code, of sorts. We didn't kill without being sure of guilt. We didn't steal from those that would be hurt by the theft. We didn't force anyone to join us. We tried to give back and protect those who were over-looked by the rest of society. Widows, orphans, the disabled."

"So there is honor among thieves after all," I said, feeling something almost like respect for him. How unexpected.

He leaned forward, his gaze intense. "Honor, yes. But your other mates are right. I was a criminal. I fought. I stole.

I killed. I am no stranger to death. That's why the Death Goddess chose me as her champion."

"You've walked away from all of that now."

"I have, but it's still a part of me. That darkness will always live in my past, and in my heart."

"I'm not afraid of the dark," I said. "But I do need to know where you stand. Will it be a problem if we face your sister again?"

"No. She's gone too far. I always knew she'd gone to some human rights rallies, and I supported that, but not this."

"I feel like such a fool. I didn't even know there were rallies about this sort of thing until recently."

"I'm sure that knowledge was kept from you. Surely you must realize now there is inequality between Dragons, humans, and elementals. Humans are defenseless against the might of the elementals, and though the Dragons now are more just than the previous ones, many still remember the old days and worry this peace won't last. The elementals or the Dragons could enslave the entire human race all too easily."

"We would never do such a thing," I said, horrified at the very idea. "The Dragons exist to keep the balance between humans and elementals, and between the four Realms. My family has no interest in ruling."

"Your grandmother ruled for hundreds of years. I know you and your parents are different now that I've met you, but before that?" He shrugged. "Many just assumed you were another set of overlords."

"That's preposterous! My parents bought peace, freedom, and prosperity to the entire world."

"And yet, the elementals still are a threat. They want more land, and humans are defenseless against them."

"Which is why they need the Dragons!" I huffed.

Varek spread his hands. "I'm only trying to show you the imbalance of power in the world. I never said it was your fault. I know you didn't ask for this role either. But in order to stop the Unseen, we must understand their purpose and why so many people are joining their ranks."

I ran a hand through my curls, tugging on them. This sort of talk was upsetting because it made me rethink everything I'd believed my entire life. Yet at the same time, it felt good to open my eyes to the truth too. If humans were suffering, it was my duty to do something about it. Even if the Unseen's methods were wrong, their message resonated with a lot of people. The imbalance of power between the elementals, humans, and Dragons had to be addressed at some point, but not with violence and murder. If the Gods would give the humans powers, or at least some of them, they could protect themselves. It might balance the world out.

But the Gods had abandoned us.

"Thank you for telling me all this," I said. "I'm glad someone can speak honestly with me about these things, and

I appreciate you telling me about your past. I feel as though I know you better now."

"And what do you think of everything I told you about my past?" His words were a challenge, but there was something vulnerable in his eyes. Whatever I said now would determine the fate of our relationship.

I stood and moved in front of him, so he had to look up at me. "I can embrace your darkness, if you will let me."

His large hands rested on my hips, sending heat to my core. "I felt it when Wrill was here, you know. I didn't hesitate coming to stop her. I couldn't let her kill you."

"Because the Death Goddess wants you to bond with me."

"Not only that." He pulled me down into his lap and rested his hand on my thigh. "Even if we weren't mates, I'd want to claim you as my own."

"Is that so?" I asked, stroking his rough jaw.

"You're smart, tough, and loyal. Not to mention, damn gorgeous. I'm too old for you, but I don't much care. You see me as a criminal and a villain, but I don't much care about that either. You will be mine."

His mouth captured mine, putting his words into action, while his fingers dug into my hips. A soft moan escaped my lips as his tongue plundered my mouth and our bodies pressed together. If I was worried about the bonding before, now all doubts fled my mind. We both wanted this, and there was no reason to wait any longer.

I pulled back and gazed into Varek's eyes. "Let's go to the Death Temple."

"Now?" he asked, as he slid his hands up my thighs.

"Do you want to wait any longer?"

"No." He set me down on the floor and stood. "No, I don't."

"Then let's get going."

CHAPTER TWENTY-ONE

The Death Temple didn't exist during my grandmother's rule. Neither did the Life Temple, for that matter. Instead, there was one place called the Spirit Temple, just south of Soulspire. That was where the battle between my parents and my grandparents was fought, and where many elementals and humans died on the field outside it. After the Spirit Goddess was split into the Life Goddess and the Death Goddess, it was decided two temples were needed. The Life Temple was built from the ruins of the old Spirit Temple, while the Death Temple was constructed on the battlefield, its powers fueled by the many lives lost in that spot. Including Varek's father.

The two temples faced one another, reflecting the twin goddesses and their never-ending rivalry. One could not exist without the other, and yet the Death Goddess had tried to take over before. She'd nearly succeeded during my grandparents' rule. My parents had sent her back to the Realm of the Dead, and she'd stayed quiet since then, at least until she demanded I take a mate to represent her too.

I'd been inside the Death Temple a few times and it had always made my skin crawl. I'd been blessed by the Life Goddess from birth, and everything about this temple was anathema to me. The building was covered in the bones of both humans and animals, and stood in the middle of the blackened and bloodstained field. Once, plants grew here and animals roamed freely, but no more.

The High Priestess Harga let us inside the temple, into a dark cavernous room lit by a single torch, which cast deep shadows across the walls. Like the exterior, the walls here were inlaid with bones of various shapes and sizes, including skulls, and in the center of the room was a statue of a huge dragon made entirely of bone too. I tried to focus on Harga instead, but her unnaturally pale skin, long black hair, and deep-set eyes only made me shiver even more.

"Welcome back, Sora. It's about time you accepted death as part of your life." Even her low voice was creepy. I forced a smile, and luckily she turned to Varek before I had to answer. "Welcome back, Varek. The Death Goddess awaits your service."

As she led us down somber, dark hallways with dry flowers, I whispered, "You've been here before?"

Varek nodded. "I came to pay my respects after being chosen."

We passed four open doorways, each with a priest standing in them, who all bowed their heads but said not a word. No food or drink was offered. No smiles were given. I felt like I was at a funeral and was vaguely worried I had not dressed for the occasion.

Harga stopped at two double doors and bowed. Then she remained in that lowered position, while we stood there. Varek opened the doors, and I followed him inside the bonding chamber, although I secretly wanted to see how long she would stay like that.

After the doors shut, Varek began to chuckle. "They're very serious here."

I blew out a long breath. "That's an understatement."

To my relief, this room didn't have any skulls or other bones on the walls. It was empty, save for a bed with black sheets and some candles. As we stepped closer, I ran my hand along the sheets. Silk.

"I have to admit, this temple managed to kill my mood from earlier, but this room is a lot better," I said.

"You said you wanted to embrace my darkness." Varek spread his arms. "Here it is."

"I didn't realize there would be quite so many skulls."

He let out a deep laugh, and then grabbed my waist and yanked me against him. When Varek looked at me, all the previous vulnerability was gone. In its place was pure lust. He kissed me hard, while his hands roamed across my body, feeling me through my long dress. He untied my cloak and let the fabric pool at my feet, while devouring my mouth like he wanted to show me he owned it.

Then he abruptly let go of me and sat on the edge of the bed, leaning back on his palms. I breathed harder, anticipation dancing up my spine.

"Now, princess..." His gaze raked down my body. "Now, you strip for me."

At first, I could only stare back at him. No one ordered me around. Not even my mates.

"Take off your clothes," he demanded.

I should have demanded he remove his own clothes. But I didn't. Something about his commanding tone made lust race through my veins. I was torn between defiance and desire. One of us had to surrender, and I realized in the Death Temple, it had to be me.

I reached up and untied the back of my dress, then slowly tugged it down my shoulders. His dark gaze devoured every inch of skin I revealed, until the fabric slid below my breasts, freeing them. Then it continued down my hips and my thighs, before pooling at my feet. I stepped out of the dress and the rest of my underthings and stood before him completely naked.

Surprisingly, it didn't embarrass me. The thought of standing naked before him excited me. Made me feel powerful even. Especially when he looked at me like the sight of my flesh was enough to drive him mad with lust.

"Aren't you going to undress now?" I asked.

"I will undress when I choose to. And you may address me as your king."

My eyes widened. Was he serious? "My king?"

"When we are alone in the bedroom together, you will call me your king." His voice left no room for argument.

I crossed my arms over my breasts. "I won't agree to that."

His lips quirked up at that. He liked when I challenged him. "You will."

Then he stood and pulled off his shirt, revealing a broad chest and strong muscles. I longed to run my hand over that skin, to feel every ridge and valley, to trace the dark hair trailing down into his trousers. Trousers which he slowly removed and slid down, revealing his perfect, very hard cock.

He rested a hand on it, knowing I was watching, then sat on the edge of the bed. "I let you win when we fought. Now I demand you fulfill your side of the bargain."

I tilted my head. "I'm not sure I believe you let me win."

"Get on your knees and suck my cock," he ordered, his eyes unforgiving.

His commands should have annoyed or infuriated me, but instead they only made me want him even more. He was the only man who could get away with saying such things to me.

I dropped to my knees, and found myself wrapping my lips around the head of his cock. I'd never taken a man into my mouth before, and though I had no idea what I was doing, I'd secretly dreamed of this moment ever since my fight with Varek. He tasted salty and masculine, and he felt huge in my mouth.

One of his hands slid into my hair, while the other he used to prop himself up on the bed. He used the grip on my hair to angle me better, as his cock slid deeper along my tongue. "That's it. Take it all, princess."

My eyes fluttered up to him, wide and unsure, and met his dark gaze. I flicked my tongue along his shaft, tasting him, and Varek grunted. Though I wasn't sure what to do, he guided me up and down on his cock, moving his hips in time to thrust inside.

"Suck harder," he said, and I tried to obey. "Good girl. Such a perfect princess, even on your knees."

Everything he said made me want him even more. How was that possible? I was desperate to please him, and even more desperate to have that cock inside me.

"Enough," he said, but I disobeyed him. I found I quite liked it now that I was getting into it. I felt powerful, knowing I could make his face twist with pleasure and elicit low grunts from his throat. He couldn't stop me—he was too far gone. His fingers tightened in my hair and he threw his head back as I sucked him harder, and his seed spurted down my throat, just like he'd demanded during our fight.

"Gods, woman. You are exquisite." He pulled his cock from my mouth and used his thumb to wipe his seed off the corner of my lips. Then he picked me up as if I weighed nothing, spun me around, and pushed me down on the bed face first. I could've fought him off, as I'd proved in the back of his bar, but I didn't want to. I was very interested in what he would do next.

His cock slid between my back cheeks, and I felt it hardening again. "None of the others have taken you here, have they?"

I shook my head, too overwhelmed to speak as his cock brushed against my tight entrance.

"Good. Tonight I'm going to fill all your holes."

With that, he thrust hard into my folds, making me gasp. I was already so wet from desire, and his cock was already slick from my mouth, that he slid inside with ease. At the same time, his finger entered my behind, turning my gasp into a loud moan. No one had touched me there before, and at first it was rather shocking, but then I liked it. Especially as he began thrusting with both his cock and his finger, pressing me down into the bed. His body completely covered mine, and I could only grip the silk sheets as he dominated me. I wanted to complain, but Gods, it felt so good to let him use my body that way.

Then he suddenly pulled out and nudged his cock into my back entrance. I nearly screamed from the intense pressure as he began to fill me from behind. It hurt, but somehow it felt good too. I didn't understand it, but I bit my lip as he kept breaching that tight hole, making me stretch around his huge shaft.

"That's it," he murmured against my hair. "Relax and let me fill you. Gods, you're tight."

Then he was suddenly completely inside, all the way to the hilt, and I felt so full I could barely stand it. He groaned as he kneaded my buttocks, letting me adjust to his size. Then he yanked up my hips, getting a better angle, so he could begin moving in and out of me.

"You're all mine now," he said, as he thrust into me. "Every inch of you belongs to me tonight."

The pressure and pain soon gave way to immense pleasure unlike anything I'd experienced before. It got even better when he slid one finger inside me, and used another to rub that sensitive spot just above my folds. All I could do was let him control my body as I braced myself on the bed, taking everything he gave me. He was rough and demanding as he claimed me, but I loved every second of it.

My orgasm came quickly and violently, making my body tremble with pleasure while sounds came out of my mouth like I'd never made before. He didn't slow. If anything, he only pounded me harder, relentless in his need to make me his own. Somehow he teased another orgasm out of me, or maybe it was the same one that only got even more intense. His cock surged inside me as his climax came too, and then darkness surrounded us in a thick layer, turning everything black. Inky shadows crawled across our bodies, tying us together, as his magic spread into me.

As soon as the darkness faded away, Varek pulled out of me and wrapped his arms around me, rolling us onto our sides so he was spooning me from behind. His hands stroked my tender skin, as his lips brushed my ear.

"I own you now, princess," he said. "But you own me too."

"My king," I whispered. "I'm yours."

His arms tightened around me as I said the word, and then he rolled me toward him. His hands cupped my cheeks, and he pressed a soft kiss to my lips. My heart fluttered faster.

"Perhaps I should call you my queen now, for you've claimed my heart as surely as I've claimed your body." He kissed me again, longer, deeper. "I never thought I could love anyone, but I love you."

I stroked his rough cheek. "I love you too. I didn't think it would be possible, but I do."

A rumbling sound interrupted our tender moment, and we both sat up, confused. Darkness seemed to crawl across the floor like fog, gathering in one spot in front of the bed, before solidifying into a large dragon made of bones. I yanked the sheets up to cover my nakedness and gasped.

The bone dragon had eyes made of darkness and decay, and she reared up and roared, spreading her skeletal wings. Varek dropped into a bow on the bed, not caring that he was naked, and I did the same while trying to retain some semblance of modesty.

"You honor us, Goddess," Varek murmured.

Of all the Gods to actually appear before me, it had to be this one. The Death Goddess fixed her beady black eyes on us and bared fangs that dripped of venom, before letting out something like a cackle. "Good work, my champion. You have mated with the Ascendant and claimed your place as one of her bonded mates."

She ignored me completely, but I straightened up and faced her, while clutching the sheet to my chest. "Why did you demand I take Varek as your mate?"

"All of the other Gods have representatives in the world. Is it not fair that I should have one of my own?"

"I suppose it is," I said. I'd never considered it that way before. "But why did you give Wrill your powers too? No God has two champions."

"I made Wrill my new High Priestess. Harga is only a decoy."

"Why?" Varek asked.

The Death Goddess swished her tail, which made a horrible clacking sound. "You both serve a purpose. Wrill's is to sow chaos and spread death, while also bringing to light the problems of this world that the other Gods have caused. Your duty is to bring balance to that chaos and continue my legacy."

Her words made no sense to me. She wanted chaos and death, but she also wanted us to stop Wrill? My parents had told me the Gods were enigmatic, but I had no idea how true that was until now.

"Even now, you think me the villain," the bone dragon said with a sneer. "Yet while the other Gods have abandoned this world, I am here."

She made a fair point, even as my heart sank. My suspicious about the other Gods were proving to be true. They could have come to give us their blessings, they simply chose not to do so.

"We will serve you as best we can," Varek said.

"See that you do." She bared her fangs. "Give my regards to my sister."

With that, the bones of her body collapsed into a heap, and then they turned to dust before our eyes. She was gone.

CHAPTER TWENTY-TWO

We spent the rest of the night alternating between sleep and sex, but in the morning, I was ready to get going. I couldn't sleep well in the temple, even if death didn't bother me as much now that I could control it—not that I planned to test that out anytime soon. More importantly, now that I'd mated with all five of my men, I could head to the Life Temple and become a dragon myself. Assuming the Life Goddess would give me her blessing.

Varek's dragon form was huge and his scales were shiny and black, like a dark lake under a moonless night. He practiced flying over the barren field around the Death Temple for a short while, before feeling confident he could fly us back the short distance to the palace.

As we approached Soulspire, we noticed other dragons flying over the city, both my parents and my mates. "A show of force?" I asked. Varek growled his agreement.

When we landed, we found the palace on lockdown, a safety measure put in place by the Silver Guard after the attacks on the city and the assassination attempt last night. My mother rushed out of the palace and glanced between me and Varek, who had already resumed his human form.

"Is it done?" she asked.

"Yes, I've bonded with all five mates," I said.

Kira then reached out her hands to Varek. "Welcome to the family. I know we got off to a rocky start, but you are one of us now."

Varek took her hands, though he looked uncertain. "Thank you."

"We want to go to the Life Temple immediately," I said.

Mom nodded. "I think that is a wise idea."

"Do you know what I should expect?"

"No. I'm sorry. Things were completely different for me. Hopefully your meeting with the Life Goddess is a lot easier."

My parents had gone to the Spirit Temple and fought my grandmother and her mates, while a huge battle was waged outside. When they'd defeated her, they'd released the Spirit Goddess and separated her into the twin Life and Death Goddesses. After banishing the Death Goddess back to her world, the Life Goddess gave Mom her blessing. I was grateful I didn't have to go through all that.

Kira wrapped me in a hug. "When you get back, we will celebrate. We're all very proud of you."

"Thanks, Mom." I gave her a squeeze and then stepped

back. She nodded at us both, and then went to speak to some of the guard.

My other mates swooped down into the courtyard, returning from their patrols of the city. I embraced them all, and felt through our bond how relieved they were that I had returned.

"How did it go?" Erroh asked.

I exchanged a glance with Varek with a secretive smile. "It went well."

"Better than well, judging by her moans," Varek said with a smirk.

My cheeks heated and I cringed a little, worried the other guys would get upset. But Carth only chuckled and said, "She does get pretty loud sometimes."

The other guys grinned and I scowled at them all. "I do not!"

That only amused them more.

"You seem different," Parin told Varek. "Lighter, somehow."

"A night with the princess will do that to a man," Varek said.

"No more of that nickname," I said, but then paused. "Unless we're in bed, anyway."

They all laughed, and I couldn't help but be amazed at the change in the group from only a week before. Even with the threat of the Unseen looming over our heads, we'd become a team. Maybe even something more.

We all freshened up and had a quick bite to eat before leaving for the Life Temple. I rode on Varek's back, surrounded by my four other dragons like an honor guard. As we flew, I thought about how this would be one of the last times I would ride on the back of a dragon—soon I would be one myself.

It was a short flight heading south of Soulspire, and soon the Life Temple came into view. The temple had been rebuilt after it had been destroyed in the battle against the Black Dragon, and unlike the Death Temple nearby, this one was surrounded by vibrant plants and animals. The temple itself sat at the top of a hill overlooking the plains, and was nestled against the side of a mountain with a waterfall running down it, which turned into a river that ran through the valley and nourished life there. The building was made of gleaming white stone, with dark green ivy wrapped around its large pillars.

The High Priestess was outside when we arrived, tending to a garden of beautiful flowers with a rabbit watching her. Nelsa was in her fifties, with very long blond hair, sun-kissed skin, and kind blue eyes. She wore a simple white gown with no sleeves and her feet were bare.

Nelsa gave me a low bow and a warm smile. "Hello, Sora. We've been expecting you. We got word you were at the Death Temple this morning."

Her priests stood at the arched doorway and gestured for us to enter. They bowed as we passed through it into an open-air courtyard with a bubbling fountain in the center topped with a dragon figure made entirely from plants. A black and white dog ran up to us and wagged its tail, while brightly colored birds perched along different spots in the courtyard and squawked loudly.

"Do you care for some refreshments?" Nelsa asked, as she led us further into the temple, the dog happily trotting beside her.

"No, thank you," I said, as I drew in a deep breath of fragrant air. Being here felt so right to me, more so than any of the other temples. I'd grown up with the Life Goddess's magic, and this place was like home.

Nelsa led us to a door on the other side of the courtyard. "The Life Goddess awaits you."

We stepped through it and were outside again in a large garden full of flowers and plants, with butterflies flitting through the air. The waterfall could be seen above us, and a stream of water gurgled nearby. A small fire pit had been set up and danced with flames, while large, smooth rocks provided seating. All of the elements were represented in this place, and it resonated deep inside me. The only one missing was death—probably because no one had planned for this fifth element to become involved.

My mates fanned out behind me, glancing around. Parin touched one of the smooth rocks. "Impressive."

Varek scowled. "I shouldn't be here."

"Nonsense," I replied, while holding out a hand. A bright blue butterfly landed on my fingertips. "You're as much my mate as any of the others."

"We're here, now what do we do?" Carth asked.

"The Life Goddess needs to be summoned," Zain said.

Erroh's face brightened. "Oh, I researched this the other week. Auric gave me some old texts. Sora needs to prove that she has all the elements, and then the Goddess shall appear and give her blessing."

"I can do that." I sucked in a breath, then took a step forward. The elemental power inside me was still fresh and new, but it was easy for me to reach. First air, from my oldest friend, Erroh. I made it swirl around me, the wind rustling my hair and dress. Next, water, from my flirtatious lover, Carth. I gathered it from the stream and made a ball of it in my palm. Third was fire, from my devoted protector, Zain. I pulled it from the fire pit and made the flames dance in my other hand. Then it was earth, from my solemn mate, Parin. I made the ground under me rumble and thrust up, lifting me above everyone else on a piece of jutting rock.

That might have done it, but I couldn't forget my final mate, Varek, even if no one had expected him. I let out a burst of death magic, making the grass under my feet shrivel up and turn brown in a circle around me.

The sun overhead seemed to brighten until it was blinding, and we all had to throw up our arms to shield our eyes.

When the light dimmed, a huge, shimmering dragon stood before us, seemingly made of light. Flowers bloomed at her feet and butterflies perched on her wings. She gazed down at me with a kind smile that filled me with warmth.

"Hello, my child," she said. "You have bonded with all of your mates and control all the elements. You are ready to become my champion."

I bowed my head, feeling breathless but also relaxed. It made no sense. "Thank you."

"I realize my sister threw in a complication, but you handled it well. I cannot fault her for wanting to be represented and worshipped as the other Gods are."

I hesitated, but then asked, "Forgive me, but where are the other Gods? We expected to meet them at their temples."

"Once your mother became the Silver Dragon, we decided to retreat from the world and let mortals control their own fates. We had so easily been corrupted and nearly led the world to ruin, we thought it would be better for our champions to guide humans and elementals into the future."

"There are many who no longer want the Dragons to lead," I said with a sigh.

"I'm certain you will find a solution to the troubles you face." She bent her head, touching my forehead with her snout like a kiss. "You have my blessing."

As soon as she touched me, she vanished. At the same time, shimmering scales rippled across my skin, while my body expanded and shifted into something much bigger. I grew claws, fangs, and a tail, then spread my sparkling wings wide. As I did, dozens of colors moved along my scales, refracting the light and forming rainbows. Pride and exultation filled my chest. I'd prepared for this moment every day of my life, and now I'd done it.

I was a Dragon, like my mother.

CHAPTER TWENTY-THREE

Flying was even better than I'd imagined all these years. Riding on the backs of other dragons was already incredible, but this topped even that. Feeling the air against my face, the strength in my body, and the power in my wings made me never want to turn human again.

I did flips and turns over the Life Temple, and my mates cheered me on while hovering beside me in their own dragon forms, while giving me a few pointers now and then. We danced in the air, chased each other around, and roared into the sky, before finally heading back to Soulspire. I couldn't wait to show my mother my new form, and to fly with my entire family.

When we arrived at the palace, I instantly knew something was wrong. Smoke filled the air, and the gate in front had been twisted and bent by someone who could control earth magic. Even worse, the bodies of slain guards were scattered across the courtyard, some blackened by fire. Other guards rushed around, shouting to one another, while palace staff tried to tend to the injured.

I shifted back to human form and grabbed the nearest guard I saw, shaking him a little. "What happened here?"

"They took them!" he sputtered, his eyes panicked.

"Who?"

"Your parents!"

Cold terror washed through me. "How? Where?"

The guard drew in a ragged breath and tried to compose himself. "Someone in the palace was working for the Unseen and poisoned your parents' meal. It knocked them out, and the Unseen attacked the palace gates and kidnapped them. We tried to stop them, but they had powers. I'm sorry."

"Where did they take them?" I nearly shouted, my heart hammering in my chest.

"I don't know!"

I turned to my mates, who had landed behind me. "We have to find them!"

"I'm the fastest," Erroh said. "I'll patrol the city while you help these people."

"I'll go too," Carth added. "I'm nearly as fast as you are, and we can cover more ground that way."

Parin nodded. "The rest of us will stay here and protect the palace and help however we can."

I wanted to protest that we should all go searching, but then I heard the moans of people in the courtyard and nodded, while choking back my fear and rage. I would be of most use here, and I trusted my mates to do the best they could to find my parents.

By the time Erroh and Carth returned, I'd managed to lose myself in the healing and block out everything else, and had done everything I could. I rushed toward my mates, eager for news of my parents.

"They're in the stadium across town," Erroh said, his voice panicked. "The Unseen are gathering a huge crowd there and they're going to drain your parents in front of everyone for all the humans to see, as soon as the sun sets. They have some elementals too. We need to go, now."

"They have those pillars up that are preventing your parents from shifting," Carth added. "Those need to be our first targets."

Gods, it was even worse than I'd thought. Especially since the sun was nearing the edge of the horizon now. I summoned water to wash the blood off my hands and then shifted back into my dragon form, enjoying the rush of power it gave me. "Let's rescue my parents and put an end to this."

"Is Wrill leading the Unseen?" Varek asked.

"Yes, she is," Carth said.

I swung my large head toward Varek. "Is this going to be a problem?"

His jaw clenched. "Not at all."

We devised a rough plan and then the five of us took off, soaring into the air as quickly as we could. This was not the time for stealth. We were going to show them that the Dragons were chosen to lead for a reason, and we would not be bullied by humans with stolen powers.

It was a short flight to the stadium on the other side of Soulspire, and we arrived just as the sun dipped below the horizon, turning the sky a deep indigo. As the six of us circled over the packed stadium, I released a loud, primal roar, laced with my anger and fear. My mates all chimed in and added their thunderous voices too, until we filled the night with the sound. Some people in the stadium screamed and began to run. Good.

The stadium was packed with onlookers, probably curious humans the Unseen had gathered to watch the event. We had to try to avoid hurting any of them. The Unseen stood in the center of the stadium, surrounding cages that held elementals and my parents, who were chained up and in their human forms. Those black pillars were set up in a circle around the cages, preventing them from shifting. Wrill stood beside one of them with her hands on her hips, gazing up at us with her face behind her black mask. I could practically feel her hatred for me even from afar.

We descended as a group, swooping down low over the crowd, sending terror throughout more people who bolted for the exit. Then we circled the center of the stadium, beating our wings rapidly. The Unseen began shooting fire, ice, and rocks up at us, while others tried to control the air around us to prevent us from flying, but we'd expected that and we fought back their attacks. Carth blasted away the fire, Zain melted through the ice, Parin defected the rocks, and Erroh soothed the wind. I helped as I could, using my elemental magic to catch anything they missed, while Varek summoned shades on the ground and ordered them to attack. We'd trained to work as a team, and even though we weren't as experienced as my parents, we were a force to be reckoned with as long as we stuck together.

While my four elemental dragons continued flying around and deflecting attacks, keeping the Unseen busy, Varek and I charged forward with our own mission. We each landed beside a pillar and placed our talons on the inky black stuff covering them, then drew out the death magic within them. The pillars collapsed, and we moved to the next ones.

"Sora!" my mother called out from inside a cage, which was also covered in that inky black stuff, probably to prevent her from using magic. My fathers were in identical cages beside her, with elementals in others behind them.

"We're going to get you out of there as soon as we can!" I roared to her, swishing my tail, then went to work on another pillar.

A huge blast of fire made me dart back. Wrill flew toward me, using air to propel herself through the sky. She attacked me with a combination of swirling air, rocks, and water, creating a hurricane that surrounded me. I threw up a shield of water and air to block it, then unleashed a massive column of fire at her. She threw out an arm and deflected the magic away from her, where it hit one of our shades and made it vanish.

She laughed as she summoned shards of ice, laced with darkness and death. "Is that all you've got?"

I let out a roar and slashed at her with my tail, but she dodged. I was about to charge her and tear her apart with my talons, but then I saw Varek behind her, back in his human form.

"I'm sorry," Varek said. "I love you, sister."

A shadowy bolt stretched out from his hand and hit her in the back, sinking into her chest. Her arms spread wide and her mask fell off as she screamed. It was just like when she'd taken the power from the elementals, but in reverse. Varek pulled out the elemental magic she'd stolen from the others with his death magic, a glowing ball of swirling colors laced with black, which dissolved into thin air before us.

When it was done, Wrill collapsed onto her knees and sobbed, then looked up at us with hateful eyes. She reached out and tried to use her magic against us, but nothing happened. She tried again and again, but it was gone. Even her death magic.

"What have you done?" she yelled.

Varek stood before her, looking down at his sister with harsh pity. "I took back what should never have been yours, and sent those poor elemental souls to the Realm of the Dead."

"You should have been one of us," Wrill said. "Our cause was just."

"Maybe so, but your methods were not." Varek tied her arms behind her, though it didn't seem like she was going anywhere now. "I believe in your cause, sister, and I will do what I can to help humans. But this is not the way."

"What other way is there?" Wrill asked, then glared at me. "If the Dragons can't help us, who will?"

Her words resonated in me, and I knew I would have to do something to address this problem soon, but not now. All around us the battle was ending, as the other Unseen members were either defeated or were surrendering to my mates. Varek and I destroyed the other pillars, then freed my parents and the other elementals.

Kira burst out of her cage and wrapped her arms around my large dragon neck. "You were incredible. And your dragon form—it's so beautiful!"

Her praise made me stand a little taller, especially as my fathers came out to hug me too. Now that they were free, it was easy to subdue the remaining attackers and throw them in the cages that once held my parents and the elementals.

Varek showed me how to remove the stolen magic inside each of the humans, and we went through them, one by one, freeing the elementals' souls. A few of the cultists might have escaped, but we'd be able to take them down if they caused any problems later.

The Unseen were no more.

CHAPTER TWENTY-FOUR

Peace was restored to Soulspire now that the Unseen were defeated, but I knew nothing will be the same. Those cultists were violent murderers and criminals, but they shed light on a real problem plaguing the world. Humans lacked the power of the elementals or the Dragons, and felt that their voices were not being heard and their lives were in danger. As the chosen representative of the Gods, it was my place to address this problem. If only I knew how.

Wrill and many of the Unseen were sent to prison. The Quickblades were disbanded. My mother called an assembly and gave a beautiful speech about change and acceptance, and though the city settled down again, I knew it wasn't enough. Real changes had to be made, or humans would rise up again to demand equality.

My mates and I settled into the palace, continuing to train together to become a stronger team, while our love grew every day. Even Varek was fitting in like a true member of the pack.

And then one night, they cornered me in my bedroom.

I had just donned my chemise when all five of my mates walked in. We had a rotating schedule set up so that I shared a bed with one man a night, plus had two nights free. This was one of my alone nights, which I often needed after being surrounded by so much masculine energy all day. However, tonight the men had other plans.

"What are you all doing here?" I asked, as they filled my room. It seemed a lot smaller with five large men inside.

"We think it's time we all took you to bed," Carth said, with a naughty gleam in his eye.

"Is that so?" It was something I'd wanted badly, but I hadn't been sure when the other men would be ready for such a thing.

"We've discussed it, and we think it would strengthen our bonds," Parin said.

Erroh rolled his eyes at his brother. "What he means is, yes, we want to do this. All of us. Together."

"Tonight," Zain said.

"Now get that chemise off," Varek demanded.

I cocked my hip. "Only if you take your clothes off too."

"I think we can manage that," Erroh said.

They were done talking then, and before I knew what was happening, they'd removed my chemise and pushed me back on the bed. For a few seconds they each took me in appreciatively, like I was the sexiest woman they'd ever seen.

Then they removed their own clothing, and it was my turn to appreciate them. Five gorgeous men, all with different muscular bodies, but each mine.

I wanted to admire their bodies some more, but they had other plans. They moved in on me as one, each taking a different section of my body. Their hands were all over me, gentle yet firm, as they explored me. Zain's fingers roamed across my calves while Carth stroked my thighs, sending waves of sweet heat right to my core. Varek's rough palms covered my breasts, squeezing and fondling them, his callused skin brushing against my nipples and making me moan. Parin's hands went into my soft hair and his mouth found mine, and we kissed while Erroh's lips moved along my neck and shoulders.

When I was first given my mates, I hadn't thought I would feel anything for Parin and Varek like what I felt for Erroh, Carth, and Zain, but as Parin kissed me, I realized I was wrong. I loved all five of them. And I wanted all five of them inside me tonight.

I pulled Erroh up to my mouth and kissed him too, while Parin moved to lick and kiss my neck. As Erroh's tongue slipped into my mouth, Carth gripped my ankles and spread my legs wide. A second later, his lips traced a path up the inside of my thighs, getting closer and closer to where I needed him. I arched my hips, wanting more, but he took his time as he got a taste of me.

Finally his mouth moved to my core and when his tongue slipped inside my wet folds, I gasped into Erroh's mouth. Parin had moved to my breasts now, sharing them with Varek, their tongues flicking against my sensitive nipples, driving me wild. I had tongues on me and inside me, worshipping me, making me feel things I'd never felt before. I was in absolute heaven.

Then Zain shoved Carth aside and dipped his head between my legs too. The two of them licked and sucked me at the same time, and I cried out when one of them lifted up my leg to get a new angle. I felt the touch of a tongue on my back hole, and all new sensations shot through me. Then the men added their fingers, sliding one of them inside each hole, and I was totally gone. The orgasm shook through me, making me cry out and grab onto the guys around me.

"That's the first of many," Carth said, as he stood up. "Tonight's all about you."

"I need you inside me," I begged. "All of you."

Varek flashed me a devilish grin. "Patience."

"We should give her what she wants," Zain said.

"Yes, she deserves it," Parin agreed. "And I'm claiming her first this time."

"Do it, brother," Erroh said.

Parin stood up and pulled me to the edge of the bed, so my behind was almost hanging off. Then he lifted my ankles and set them on his shoulder, exposing me and stretching me wide. I was shocked at his boldness, but Parin had changed a lot during our time together.

"Beautiful," he said, as he gripped his cock and rubbed it

against my wetness. Then he grabbed my behind and lifted my hips up as he pushed inside. "This what you want?"

"Yes!"

He pulled my hips flush against his, and he was buried so deep in me thanks to this angle. He held onto my ankles as he began sliding in and out, withdrawing almost completely, them slamming back inside in one hard thrust.

The other four men were watching with lusty eyes, and I knew they would want to get in on this soon. I reached for Erroh and he moved toward me, bringing that long cock right by my face. I took it in hand and brought it to my mouth, humming in approval as he slipped inside. I licked and sucked on his hard length, until he closed his eyes in satisfaction, while his brother pumped into me. Varek pinched my nipples at the same time, sending a touch of pain to mingle with the pleasure. I moaned around Erroh's cock and he dug his fingers into my hair, moving my head as he thrust between my lips. Then he surged against my tongue and his hot seed spilled down my throat. Parin pumped into me harder as he came at the same time, and seeing both brothers come apart sent me over the edge too.

"Our turn," Carth said.

I didn't have time to recover before Zain was lifting me up, wrapping my legs around his waist. He turned so he could lay back on the bed with me on top of him with his cock in me, nice and deep. I liked being on top and I began to ride him, my breasts hanging over his face. Carth moved behind and grabbed my cheeks, then spread them wide. I felt some oil being slid into my back entrance, followed by the pressure of his cock there.

"We're both going to be in you at once," Carth said, his lips by my ear. "Do you want that?"

"Yes!" I managed to get out, as the feeling became overwhelming. Carth pushed inside to the hilt, filling me completely, while his best friend filled me from the front.

Carth had his hands on my hips, and he guided himself in and out of me, which pushed me on and off Zain at the same time. Soon they found a rhythm and all I could do was give myself up to it, as the pleasure built quickly.

"I need to get in there too," Varek said, and then his cock was shoved between my lips so fast and hard I almost gagged. Somehow when Varek treated me roughly like that it only turned me on even more. I looked up at him with a challenge in my eyes as he pumped into my mouth, but I was helpless to do anything but let him own me.

Varek grabbed my chin and held me steady as the other guys pounded into me from behind and below. Their skin was touching me everywhere, and I didn't know where any one of us ended and the other began. We were one entity, writhing in pleasure together, racing toward our release.

It was too much though, and soon I was screaming around Varek's cock as the most amazing orgasm exploded through my body. That caused both Carth and Zain to climax into me with quick thrusts and rough groans, their fingers digging into my skin. I thought Varek might do the same, but instead he lifted me off the other men, wrapped my legs around his waist, and slid his cock into me. I was already weak from pleasure and could only hold onto him and enjoy the lingering effects of my climax as he came inside me too, while kissing me hard.

When it was over, we all collapsed in the bed, a mess of sweaty limbs and pounding hearts. I understood now why this bed was so large and smiled up at the ceiling. My soul was bursting not just with pleasure, but with love.

"That was incredible." I touched each of their faces softly. "I love you all so much."

"We love you too," Erroh said, and the other guys murmured in agreement as they curled up around me and pressed loving kisses to my skin.

Varek propped himself up on one muscular arm. "Now that we've all filled you with our seed, can we expect a child in nine months?"

I gave him a sad smile. "It doesn't work that way. In ten years, I will have one daughter, who will become the next Ascendant. No more, no less. Such is the price we pay as Dragons."

Erroh idly rubbed my stomach with his hand. "How do we determine who the father will be?"

"I'm putting in my claim now," Varek said.

Parin played with my curls. "I don't think that's allowed."

"No, we'll have some sort of contest when the time comes," Carth said.

"What kind of contest?" Zain asked.

"We're not having a contest," I said, but a pang hit my heart at the thought of not having a child with each of them. I wanted that, more than I could ever imagine.

Then I had an idea.

I untangled myself from my men and stood up, gathering my clothes. "Get up. We're going to the Life Temple."

Erroh sat up with a confused expression. "Now?"

"Why?" Zain asked.

"Because I know how to fix things."

CHAPTER TWENTY-FIVE

High Priestess Nelsa was very confused by our sudden arrival at the temple in the middle of the night, but she couldn't refuse us either. With a yawn, she led us to the outside area where we had met the Life Goddess before, and then bowed and left us alone.

Once there, I stood in front of my mates and centered myself. I'd never summoned the Gods before, but the old tomes all said it was possible. They were just vague on how exactly.

Focusing on my power, on the magic deep inside me, I pulled the elements out. The twin forces of life and death, along with fire, water, air, and earth. Tugging on each thread, they erupted from my fingers with a rush of color. Wrestling with them, I forced the colorful magical threads to comply, and weaved them around one another, moving my arms to help me focus my mind until they were braided together. Then I released the magic into the world.

"I call on the Gods to appear before us!" I yelled, as I pushed my power into the fabric of the realm, into the very source of it all. The primal essence of the universe.

My mates then released a burst of their own magic and called out to the Gods, and through our bond I felt their power surging and strengthening mine. We were all connected, with invisible chains tying us together, and through that bond I demanded the Gods appear before us.

And then, they did. First the Life Goddess, in her radiant glory, her dragon scales erupting with light. Beside her stood the Death Goddess, with her bones and poison fangs. Then the four male Gods appeared behind them, all of them in their dragon forms. The Fire God, with skin like shifting lava and flames on his breath. The Earth God, massive in size and made entirely of crystal. The Water God, composed of shifting waves with talons of ice. The Air God, with cloudy wings and lightning in his eyes.

"You have summoned us and we have appeared," the Life Goddess said. "What do you require, child?"

I glanced at my mates, and several of them nodded, giving me strength. I straightened up and faced the Gods. "You said the Gods wished to retreat from the world and let mortals control their own destiny. Is this still true?"

"Yes, it is," the Earth God said, his voice like the rumbling of a rockslide.

"We brought much chaos and pain to the world when we were corrupted," the Air God rasped.

The Fire God flexed his flaming wings. "We will not allow that to happen again."

"We have faith in our champions to lead the mortal world," said the Water God, whose tail swished, spraying drops everywhere.

"You made this world," I said. "And now you plan to abandon it?"

"No," the Life Goddess replied. Her smile sent hope and joy searing through my heart. "We'd never leave it. We will still be there, but more as silent observers."

"Including the Death Goddess?" I asked.

She snarled and bared her fangs. "I have done what was required to bring necessary changes to this world. Now I am content to rule the Realm of the Dead."

I bowed my head. "If you plan to remove yourself from this world, then I have a few requests for things that would bring balance to the world. That is my purpose, after all."

"Name them," the Life Goddess said.

"Give all mortals elemental powers and the ability to turn into dragons."

"That is too much power," the Fire God roared with a rush of heat.

"Agreed," the Water God said, his voice laced with frost.

Lightning crackled in the Air God's eyes. "Humans can be troublesome and combative."

"If they all had magic it would lead to never ending wars," the Earth God rumbled.

I had a feeling they would say something like that, and I was prepared with an answer. "Then give the power only to a few select humans who embody the traits you each look for in your own champions. Bravery, wisdom, and so forth. Then allow the power to pass down to their children."

The Gods all glanced between one another, and I sensed they were communicating telepathically. Some time passed, and I shifted on my feet, nervous they wouldn't agree to my proposal. If this failed, I had no other plan for helping the humans.

"Very well," the Life Goddess finally said. "We will choose the humans who will become our champions, and the ability will be passed down through their lineage. But be prepared. As with other things, the humans may not always make the best choices with their magic."

"If we do this, it will mean the end of the Ascendancy," the Death Goddess said. "You and your Dragons will no longer be the only champions of the Gods. Are you ready to make that sacrifice?"

I sucked in a breath. "I am. As long as you allow me to have as many children as I wish, and promise they will be no different than any other of your other champions."

"Very well," the Life Goddess said. "You will be the last Ascendant."

She reached out with one of her claws and touched my

chest lightly. I felt a shiver run through me. Otherwise, I felt no different.

"It is done." She raised her wings. "Our champions will be chosen by dawn. They will require your guidance. Be prepared."

I nodded and swallowed hard. This would be a new challenge, but one my mates and I would be ready to face— and it would bring balance to the world.

EPILOGUE

ONE YEAR LATER

I paced back and forth in the chamber, biting my nails, while the train of my long silver gown trailed behind me.

Erroh swatted at my hand. "Stop that."

I dropped it and clutched my rumbling stomach instead. "I'm going to be sick."

"You're going to be fine," Parin said, in his calm, firm voice.

Carth wrapped an arm around my shoulders. "Relax, Sora. This is your day. Well, all of ours, really."

"It's just so much responsibility," I said.

"Your parents wouldn't be doing this if they didn't feel it was right," Zain said.

Varek took my hand and pressed a kiss to it. "You're going to do great."

The door opened, and my four fathers stood on the other side. Like me and my mates, they were dressed in their finest clothes, each one in the color representing their element.

"It's time," Jasin said, before giving me a warm hug.

I stepped back, shaking my head. "I'm not ready."

"Yes, you are," Reven said, as he stroked my hair. "We've trained you for this since the moment you were born."

"I'm not, though," I said. "I have so much to learn still. What if I make a mistake?"

"You did a wonderful job dealing with the cult," Auric said, as he squeezed my hand. "And it's not like we're going to disappear. We'll always be here to guide you and advise you."

"True." I smoothed my dress, gathering my confidence, but it only returned when Slade wrapped me in one of his big bear hugs.

"We're very proud of you," he said.

Tears pricked my eyes as I pulled back and looked at my four fathers. Things might have been awkward with them and my mates at times, especially at first, but I could never have asked for four better men to raise me. Each one of them had given me the best parts of themselves and loved me unconditionally. I owed them everything—along with my mother, of course.

We stepped out of the palace and into the courtyard, which was filled with people as far as the eye could see, along with elementals. Kira stood in a silver gown of her own on a podium, with her sword in her hand, the one Slade had made her that was imbued with all the elements. My fathers moved to fan out behind her, and then my mates and I stood to the side.

Mom flashed me a warm smile, as the sunlight glinted off her beautiful red hair. Then she turned to the crowd.

"For thousands of years the Dragons have acted as guardians, protectors, and sometimes overlords of the world, but our time has come to an end. My daughter, the Rainbow Dragon, shall be the last of the Ascendants, and shall oversee the beginning of a new era. She has brought balance to the world, and has made a great sacrifice to ensure that equality shall flourish among all mortals."

The crowd watched with rapt attention, and my heart warmed at the sight of so many familiar faces. Erroh and Parin's parents, Faya and Cadock, along with their sister and her family. Carth's parents, Brin and Leni. All of the High Priestesses from every temple, including Calla. Even a few former members of the Quickblades, who had joined the Silver Guard at Varek's request.

Kira lifted up her sword and turned toward me. "Sora, you and your mates have proven yourselves ready to take on the peaceful oversight of our world. My mates and I formally step aside, and we charge you with keeping the harmony between humans and elementals, and maintaining balance in the four Realms."

I took the sword from her and bowed my head as I held its weight. "I take on this duty with pride and honor, with my mates by my side."

The audience erupted into cheers as I sheathed the sword, and my mother and I faced the crowd, our men behind us. Mom rested a hand on my back and gave me a proud smile that brought tears back to my eyes. Kira and her men were not only heroes, but amazing parents too. I could only hope to live up to the example they'd set.

The ceremony ended, and a banquet began. A small orchestra began to play music, and food and refreshments were served to the guests. The night quickly passed in a whirlwind of drinking, dancing, and delicious food. Everyone wanted to congratulate me and my mates, and ask us about the new school we'd found just outside Soulspire, the Elemental Dragon Academy.

Ever since the night we summoned the Gods, humans across the four Realms had woken up to new powers. Most of the champions were young, below twenty, but a few of them were older. We sent out word that anyone with magic should come to Soulspire for training, and for weeks we flew around the world, looking for our new students and transporting them to their new home. My family built it from scratch using magic, and it would house hundreds of people. We asked the High Priestesses, both former and current, to help us with the training, along with my parents. So far, it was going well. The new dragons were smaller and less powerful than we were, but they gave the people hope. That was what mattered.

Our purpose now was to train the next generation of elemental dragons and to create a school that would continue after we had moved on. Especially since our own children would need to be trained there too.

I found my mates in my mother's garden, my favorite place at the palace. They all turned toward me and smiled as I approached, and I decided now was the time to tell them the good news.

"What are you doing out here?" I asked.

"Getting away from all the stuffy guests with a million questions," Carth said with a smirk.

"Yes, it's much quieter out here," Parin said.

"Wine?" Varek offered me, with a knowing gleam. "I noticed your glass has been empty all night."

"No, thank you," I said, as I sat on a bench. "There's something I need to tell you all."

Erroh's face lit up. "We already know."

"You do?" I asked.

"It's obvious from the way you've been acting," Zain said. "You're pregnant."

I laughed and placed a hand over my belly. "How could you tell? I wasn't even sure myself until Mom examined me this morning."

"No wine or ale was the obvious one, of course," Carth said.

"Additionally, you refused eggs for breakfast, and we know you love eggs," Parin added.

"And you kept complaining of being tired," Zain said.

Carth smirked. "I suppose that means we don't need to have a competition over who will be the father. This time, anyway."

"Do you know who it is?" Erroh asked.

I bit my lip, but then nodded, and my gaze landed on Varek. His eyes widened in shock, and then he let out a laugh. Next thing I knew, he was sweeping me up into his arms and giving me a passionate kiss.

"It's mine? Truly?" he asked.

"Yes, Mom confirmed it with her magic," I said. "A boy too. The first boy ever born to any Ascendant."

He pressed his forehead against mine and laughed again. "I can't believe it. We're going to have a son."

The other men patted him on the back and congratulated him, but I wanted to make sure they understood something important. I turned to my mates and said, "Even though Varek is the biological father, this child shall be son to all of you. As will any other children we have. Just like my parents raised me."

"I claim the next one," Erroh said, and everyone laughed. I rolled my eyes, knowing he wasn't serious. Probably.

We hugged and kissed and laughed until the party disbanded, and then we returned to our wing of the palace together. Tomorrow we'd head back to the academy to work with the students, but tonight we would relax. Satisfaction and happiness settled upon me as I climbed into my large bed with my five men. The four Realms were at peace again, and I was starting a family with the men I loved.

Though the time of the Dragons would soon be over, our legacy would live on. Forever.

ABOUT THE AUTHOR

New York Times Bestselling Author Elizabeth Briggs writes unputdownable romance across genres with bold heroines and fearless heroes. She graduated from UCLA with a degree in Sociology and has worked for an international law firm, mentored teens in writing, and volunteered with dog rescue groups. Now she's a full-time geek who lives in Los Angeles with her family and a pack of fluffy dogs.

Visit Elizabeth's website: www.elizabethbriggs.net

Printed in Poland
by Amazon Fulfillment
Poland Sp. z o.o., Wrocław

61007690R00136